To Pat.

With love from
Barbara.
25. 12. 1928.

The Little Green Road to Fairyland

SHE SAW A GREEN MOSSY WALL, AND IN IT
A LITTLE GREEN MOSSY DOOR.

The Little Green Road to Fairyland

By
Annie R. Rentoul
and
Ida Rentoul Outhwaite

A. & C. Black Ltd
4, 5 & 6 Soho Square London, W.1.
1925

First published September, 1922.

To

ALL WHO LOVE FAIRIES

AND HAVE FOUND

THE LITTLE GREEN ROAD

SHINY Eyes at dawn of day
  In the daisies playing
Found a little shy green way
  Through the meadow straying;
Shiny Eyes could understand
  All its grassy pleading:
"Follow me to Fairyland,
  Whither I am leading."

Shiny Eyes at set of sun,
  When the stars were peeping,
Saw a little twinkly one
  Very near come creeping;
Gaily took its golden hand,
  Toys of earth forsaken,
Followed far to Fairyland,
  Where sweet dreams awaken.

Printed in Great Britain

CONTENTS

Contents

IN COLOUR

IN BLACK AND WHITE

THE LITTLE GREEN WAY

LONG, long ago,
　　When I was six or seven,
I thought the golden stars aglow
　　Were peepholes out of Heaven.

I thought the daisies white
　　My love and kisses knew,
And, if I did not say good-night,
　　Their eyes would fill with dew.

The bunnies soft and shy,
　　The flittermouse on wings,
The little sweet blue wren and I
　　Alike were elfin things.

The way to Fairyland,
　　The little shy green way,
I thought was very close at hand
　　To wander in all day.

So long ago
　　Those golden summers seem,
I wonder were they really so,
　　Or just a sunlit dream.

But still sometimes
　　"Hush!　Hush!" I whisper low,
And listen for the Fairy chimes,
　　As *we* did long ago.

Then sweet and clear
　　Ring back the bells of gold,
And Fairyland once more is near,
　　And we are seven years old.

THE
LITTLE GREEN ROAD TO FAIRYLAND

Prologue

ROBIN and Maykin nodded their heads together like a little buttercup and daisy. They were weaving wild-flower chains and talking about Fairies. Often and often they caught the flash of Fairies peeping and popping in and out among the grass. Fairies are the *quickest* things, quicker than a star in the sky, a fish in a pool, a dimple in your cheek, or a thought in your mind.

"I wish we could see one *properly !*" said Maykin.

"But they won't keep still a minute !" sighed Robin. "They are so busy. What are they doing ?"

"Lovely, lovely things !" said Maykin. "They waken baby buds, paint butterflies' wings, uncurl the ferns, and dance in our hearts to make us glad."

"But how do they come ? Do they just happen out in the air like stars ?"

"Oh, no !" said Maykin. "God makes everything, and He makes Fairies to help Him with the little things, because He is so busy with the big things. Look,

look, there is one now! I thought it was a wild violet!"

Robin was just in time to see the violet float away on filmy wings till it was lost in the blue of the sky.

But now it was tea-time. The evening star had lit her lamp, the cowbells tinkled homeward, the daisies were closing their drowsy eyes and the birds folding their wings on the nest. Indoors at the farm Robin and Maykin knelt beside their little white beds and prayed: "Please, God, show us a Fairy soon."

And while they slept the Fairies were weaving round them a ring of strange and wondrous flowers. These are the dream-flowers, frailer far and lovelier than our earth-blossoms. They have radiant petals and gold or silver leaves all made of moonlight and sunshine. Whom the Fairies love, they circle with these flowers. But to pluck them, ah, that is the trouble! Often little children do, but seldom grown-ups can. They are too blind to see the flowers, and they crush and trample them underfoot, and break the magic ring. Robin and Maykin woke with shiny eyes and wise hearts. Now listen, and you shall hear their adventures.

The Fairy

Chapter 1

The Fairy

"Come away, O human child!
To the waters and the wild
With a fairy, hand in hand."
W. B. YEATS.

HAVE *you* ever seen a Fairy? If not, open your eyes wide and believe you will see one, and you will be sure to soon. Not all Fairy tales happened once upon a time. This story happened to Robin and Maykin last summer. Any day a Fairy tale may come to *you*; *you* may be a Fairy Prince or Princess, and kill a big fiery dragon, or ride on a horse with wings, find the golden apple-tree and the valley of diamonds, or sail to foreign parts on a magic carpet.

Robin and Maykin were just a little boy and girl like you. They lived among the mountains in the Land of Gums at Tranquillity Farm. It was a sweet old home, with a dear old garden full of roses, and lilies, and lavender; brown bees, white doves, singing birds; shady trees, red-tiled paths, little silver streams hurrying through the grass. There were golden cornfields, an orchard with rosy apples and brown nuts, and out in the paddocks, mushrooms and blackberries. It was just the sort of farm children love, with cows, horses, lambs, chickens, and all sorts of pets. From the wide honeysuckle-bowered veranda one could see, beyond the plainlands far away, the blue line of the ocean.

Beyond the home-paddocks were the forest and the

3

fern-gully. Down in the gully Fairyland began.
There Robin and Maykin loved to play and wander;
there things happened. It was always Fairytime in the
gully, and that meant you need never bother about late
and early, but just dream along in the cool shadows
and golden sun. You could splash with bare feet under
the tree-ferns in the crystal creek, lie on the mossy
stones to watch the baby trout breathing with their fins
in the clear brown pools, and listen to the stream's
laughing song. When you went home, it was always
early for tea, unless a naughty elf sometimes made the
puff o'clocks go too fast.

Across the gully in a forest-clearing stood the
woodcutter's little homestead. Robin and Maykin
loved the woodcutter's wife, who made them johnny-
cakes and knew all about the Fairies. Once she had
had a sweet baby girl called Lily, but Lily had gone
away to Heaven, and the woodcutter and his wife
were sad and lonely without her. It seemed such a
long time till they should see her again.

In the forest there was a little Fairy. She was
the very one Robin and Maykin saw among the daisies.
She flew one sunny day from Fairyland to waken a
bank of wild violets. Her wings were shimmery,
frail, and almost too beautiful to see, and often that
is why we cannot see Fairy things. They are too
beautiful and we are too blind.

The violets loved the Fairy, and begged her to live
with them a little while. They gave her honey to eat
and dew to drink. "You shall be our child," they

"I AM KEXY, FRIEND TO FAIRIES."

The Fairy

said. So Fairy lived with the wild violets. If a mortal passed along, she just turned into a violet and hid. She could fly away, too, on wings, like a butterfly. In fact, she could do just anything she liked; for, you know, Fairies *can*.

All the same, it was a little dangerous for Fairy at first, before the wild things knew her. One day, when she was a butterfly resting on the violets, a big green frog nearly gobbled her up. She *did* scare him when she quickly turned into a Fairy.

"Croak, croak, croak! Who are you? I am Kexy, friend to Fairies, foe to flies."

"I am Fairy. Please be my friend!"

"Well, Fairy, it's better that I did not swallow you. One never knows the effect of strange food, and Fairy *would* be rather unusual. Let us be friends, and I promise not to do it again. Come for a swim across the pool."

So Fairy rode on Kexy's back, and he steeple-chased over logs and rushes, and it was a glorious ride.

Soon all the creatures of the Bush and gully and creek grew to love Fairy. She was the darling of the forest.

One day, when Fairy was flying about, she came to the woodcutter's little cabin in the clearing. "I must be careful," she thought, "for this house has such glittering eyes. Maybe the wicked gnomes live here that lose children in the wild woods."

She flew nearer, and the cabin's glass eyes began to sparkle at her in a friendly way, for there was firelight within. "I will look right into your eyes, deep down to

5

your heart," thought Fairy. So she peeped in at the window. There was a mug of daisies on the table, and the woodcutter's wife was laughing and cutting bread-and-jam for a little boy and a little girl, who were Robin and Maykin. They were laughing too, and looking up in her face. She had the shiniest of eyes you ever saw.

"I will fly nearer," thought Fairy, "and hear all they are saying!"

She tried to push her way through the window-pane, but it was hard and cold, and she could not get in. The tiny fluttering noise of her wings on the glass made the woodcutter's wife and the children look round.

"Oh, oh!" cried Robin, running to the window. "What a lovely butterfly! It's just like a violet. Let's catch it for school."

"No, no!" said Maykin. "Let it fly away! You will brush all the dust off its wings and maybe kill it."

"Hush, hush!" said the woodcutter's wife, whose name was Mary Love. "Why, children, it's a *Fairy!*" Her eyes were shinier than ever. "Do not try to catch her. Fairies are so shy and wild. Oh, the sweet little thing!"

Now when Fairy heard this her little heart grew all warm and throbby with love and joy. She felt she would do *anything* for Mary Love. Robin had thrown the window wide open, and Fairy flew right in and circled round and round looking at everything. She sipped the milk, tasted the jam, and perched on a daisy and had a good look at her new friends.

They could all see now quite plainly that she was

6

really and truly a Fairy. Robin was a little scared, Maykin was too happy to speak or move, and Mary Love was just smiling and smiling and not saying anything. Fairy danced for them and sang for them—loud as a cricket and sweeter than a bluebonnet—but when she thought she would like another taste of jam, the tip of one gossamer wing got caught in it, and Mary Love had great trouble helping her out with a daisy-stalk, so as not to crush her frail little wing. This adventure alarmed Fairy very much. She flew right out of the open window home to the violet-bank, without saying good-bye or thank you. It certainly was a frightening adventure. How would you like to sink down in a big pool of jam? You couldn't even *eat* any. Kexy and the violets were thrilled to hear about it.

Chapter 2

Mary Love

" Children have no greater blessing than their mother. Children, love your mother, for no love is so strong, so sweet, as that between a mother and a child."—EURIPIDES.

FAIRY knew she had been ungrateful. She made up her mind to go back and say thank you. Really she wanted to see Mary Love again. Somehow she could not keep away from her shiny eyes and the lovely look in them. It was so gentle and dear.

One evening she flew back to the forest-clearing. She peeped through the window, but no one was inside.

The Little Green Road to Fairyland

The room had a lonely look, though logs blazed cheerily on the hearth. Fairy flew all round the clearing seeking Mary Love.

Soon she found her kneeling beside a little green hillock where a tall lily grew. There was a little wooden cross on the hillock, and " Lily " written there. Mary was crying, and the big tears frightened Fairy.

" What shall I do ?" she thought. " This is too sad for a Fairy !" She perched on Mary's clasped hands and fluttered her wings to let her know she was there. She kissed her hands too, and a Fairy's kiss is very sweet. Mary looked down and smiled. But it was a sad smile, and Fairy's little heart was nearly breaking. Her shimmery wings were all dull and crumply with sympathy.

" I cannot stay here !" she thought. " A Fairy must have joy and sunlight. I should die if I stayed here. I will fly away, and forget all about it."

Off she flew to the violet-bank, and left Mary all alone. But that night she could not dance with the moonbeams. She crept under a violet-leaf and was just miserable. She made all the violets cry, and Kexy sobbed dismally in the pool. The mopoke kept hooting all night, and Fairy grew sadder and sadder. For she could not forget Mary, and yet she could not make up her mind to become a little earth child and live with Mary in the woodcutter's cabin.

At dawn the sunbeams woke her to go and play with them. The kookaburras were laughing and the world was full of fun. Fairy flew high up in the golden

8

ONE EVENING SHE FLEW BACK TO THE FOREST-CLEARING

air, as far and as fast as she could, over the tree-tops. Soon her troubles were forgotten. " What care I," she thought. " I will be wild and free." She danced about faster and faster in the air. Far down below she could see Mary's cabin, but it looked a very little thing, too little to worry about.

When Fairy was tired, she rested on a spray of gum-blossom. She was having lovely times, for earth was so new to her after Fairyland, and there were all kinds of curious things to discover.

" I will pull the lid off this little bud," she thought, "and see what happens." So she pulled off the little cap, and out came a white gum-blossom and stretched its crumpled petals in the sunlight. " What fun !" said Fairy. " I will fly further and see what next." She flew to another gum-tree top, and down below lay the woodcutter's cottage. Just then in the ferns below there was a flash, a blaze, a dreadful noise, which echoed all through the forest. On the ground a sweet little fluffy bunny lay still and dead. It was all done by a rabbiter with his bang-fire stick.

Fairy stroked the bunny's soft fur, and whispered in his ear to wake up ; but it was too late. For the real bunny had gone to Fairyland, and it was only a bunny's fur and bones lying there.

Now Fairy thought it was time to fly home to the violets, for her adventures to-day were far too exciting. " I will peep at Mary for the last time on my way home," she said. She alighted in the garden of the cottage, and, as Mary was not about, began to explore.

The Little Green Road to Fairyland

There was a snug little barn in one corner of the yard. Fairy peeped in. "I wonder who lives here?" she thought. "Really the world is full of things to see!" On a heap of golden straw in a box lay some lovely white eggs. "I will just chip one and see what happens," said Fairy.

She tapped an egg-shell, and suddenly there was a loud crack and a monstrous yellow chicken walked out —at least it seemed monstrous to Fairy—and cheeped, pecked, and made a snap at her. What a fright she got! She did not wait for the chicken to explain that he only wanted to say "How do you do?"; he was really a kind and jolly little fellow. But Fairy thought earth was very dangerous, and back she flew into the gum-tree.

But there she saw a terrible thing. The woodcutter had ring-backed and killed a dear old gum-tree, the friend of all the forest. As he was felling it with his axe, the sprite of the gum-tree pushed it over on him in revenge, and the woodcutter was lying dead beside the fallen gum-tree in the clearing. It was not the gum-tree's fault. He had lived near Heaven so long that he had learned gentle ways. But the little sprite living in the gum-tree was angry and resentful, and *he* had killed the woodcutter.

"Oh, what will become of Mary now?" cried poor little Fairy. "I cannot bear to think of it. I will fly away and forget." But she could not forget; she could not rest happy because of Mary's eyes all dim with tears. At last she did a very brave thing for a

WHAT A FRIGHT SHE GOT!

chief difference : now she had a mortal heart. Do you know what that means for a Fairy ? She could never fly back to Fairyland till she lost the mortal heart and found the Fairy one again. Only the Fairy Queen knew where the Fairy heart was hidden, and our little Fairy would have to discover the secret before she could win back her Fairy heart. When Fairy decided to become a mortal child, suddenly, like a shooting star, a mortal heart, rose-red and glowing, whizzed into her, on flame-coloured wings, and her Fairy heart, frail as a snowflake and shimmering like a rainbow, whizzed off to Fairyland, and the Fairy Queen had hidden it somewhere. A Fairy's heart, you know, is like a tiny bubble, so frail and delicate and iridescent. It will break almost if you look at it. But a mortal heart, if it is a true one, pulses braver and stronger the harder it is used. Fairy could not have lived a child on earth without a mortal heart. It was a big risk too that she might never find her Fairy heart at all, nor get home in the end to Fairyland. The silver key of earth was tied round her neck on a little frail chain, but where was the golden key to Fairyland ? That too was hidden somewhere, and Fairy must find it before she could fly home. Other Fairies can fly to and from Fairyland when they wish, but not our Fairy. She must stay on earth as long as she was a mortal child. So now she was lost in the Big World, till she found her Fairy heart and her golden key again. It was just as if a child were marooned on a desert island.

"I must make the best of things now," thought

The Fairy Child

wise little Fairy, and she blinked hard and looked at Mary's lovely eyes. "Anyway, there are all sorts of new things to see and know and do." She was a lucky baby, for she understood Fairy-talk, baby-talk, mortal-talk, flower-talk, and the speech of all the wild creatures of the Bush. You see, she was a Fairy. "It is really lovely to be a baby and have a mother," Fairy said. "I am very cosy so far."

Mary was, of course, a little surprised at the Fairy toys the baby brought with her. But she unfastened the wings where they were fitted into the dimples on Fairy's shoulders, and folded them neatly away with the flute and the wand and the silver key in a cupboard. She could not, of course, see Fairy's heart, but she noticed her beautiful eyes just like two dewy violets. "I will call her Violet," said Mary, and Fairy smiled to show she was pleased with the name.

What fun she had in her first bath! But how surprised she was that all the bubbles burst when she caught them! Why, Fairy bubbles are as strong as diamonds and never break! "I am getting to like the bursty sort," said Fairy. "They are more exciting and harder to catch. There goes a lovely one! Puff! It's out!"

The violets and Kexy had an anxious time when Fairy vanished. They thought a spider had caught her, or a kookaburra gobbled her up by mistake, or something dreadful. But while Mary was asleep at night, Fairy crawled to the cupboard (she was a Fairy, you know, as well as a baby), got her wings, and flew off to the forest pool. Have you ever seen a little fat baby flying on wings? It is funny but sweet. Fairy soon told her story, and the violets thought she was right to stay with Mary; but Kexy was a little vexed.

"You were ours first," he said.

"I shall love you just the same," said Fairy; "and you shall see me just as often. You may come and live with us, and I will visit my darling violets every day."

Just then Fairy heard a cock crow, which is the time for Fairies to fly to Fairyland. This was the first time she had stayed on earth at cockcrow, and she *did* feel queer. She flew home, crept in at the window, snuggled under the coverlet of her cradle, and tried to think things out.

Chapter 4
Gumkin

"And the Elves also,
Whose little eyes glow,
Like the sparks of fire, befriend thee."
HERRICK.

NOW we must remember Robin and Maykin at the farm. One day they planned to go and look for Fairies across the gully. "Take this basket, then," said Mother, "to Mary Love. She must be very lonely without her husband and baby. Carry it carefully; there are eggs and butter and a pot of cream." She gave Robin the basket, and Maykin a

THE BROWNIE WAS VERY BRAVE NOW.

Gumkin

big posy of sweet flowers. Then she kissed the children good-bye, and they set out for the gully.

It was very hot and the basket was heavy. In the gully the children sat down to rest on the mossy stones under a big tree-fern. The murmuring of the creek and the cicadas drumming on their tiny drums made them drowsy, and they fell asleep. Maykin was wakened by a tiny rustling noise in the ferns. It was not the breeze whispering, nor a goanna stirring the brambles, but a naughty little Brownie with great green eyes and a feather in his round cap. He was dipping his finger in and out of the cream-pot and licking it, not a very polite thing to do, but one hardly expects good manners in a Brownie. Brownies are not so well brought up as the other Fairy-folk. A little way off sat troops and troops of other Brownies with watering mouths and streaming eyes; they longed to taste the cream, but did not dare to come near enough, and at the rate their comrade was polishing it off, soon it would all be gone. So they just whimpered and chattered like tiny monkeys, and sorrowfully watched the cream disappearing.

Maykin ought to have said " Shoo !" Instead she said "Sh!" and gave Robin a gentle push to wake him.

The Brownie was very brave now. He was lapping up the cream with his little pink tongue like a kitten. Soon he put his whole head into the jar, and there it stuck fast, and he began to spin round and round in an agony of terror with the cream-pot on his head like a helmet. The other brownies scattered in dismay with

15

shrill squeals like parrakeets and left their leader to his doom.

With difficulty Robin caught the Brownie, and gently pulled the cream-pot off his head; but instead of gratitude, he bit Robin's finger with his sharp little white teeth. Have you ever had a Brownie bite? It is worse than the sting of a bee. Robin was just about to give the Brownie a good hard smack, but he looked such a tiny drowned ghost, pale and dripping with cream, that he had not the heart. "Why did you do that?" he asked reproachfully while Maykin dried the Brownie with her handkerchief, scolding all the time. "You graceless, shameless, heartless scamp! Now my Robin will die of blood-poison!"

"Not at all," said the Brownie airily. "*That* sting was not poisonous! Would you like to try a real poison sting?"

"*You* stand there," said Maykin sternly, setting him on a stone in the middle of the running water. "If you dare to move, we will throw you to the fish in the stream. You couldn't get out—and very well you know it—if once your wings were drenched."

The Brownie was a good deal sobered, and, when Robin asked, told him meekly enough that he was Gumkin, the Brownie Chief.

"I am willing to be friends and make a truce," he said magnanimously.

"Yes, but you began the quarrel," said Robin.

"I also end it," said Gumkin, puffing himself out pompously. "If you children care, we Brownies will form your bodyguard and go with you everywhere. It would be useful, for we can always become invisible at pleasure."

" That will be useful," said Robin to Maykin. " We will take them to school. Think of the fun !"

Maykin clasped her hands and danced for joy to think of it.

" We accept your offer," Robin said gravely, " but only on condition you obey orders. Breach of orders means expulsion for ever."

" Agreed !" said Gumkin. " I'm off to tell the Boys." He vanished into the forest like a grasshopper, and the children went on their way to Mary Love's.

Chapter 5

Robin and Maykin Meet the Fairy

"Thou, whose exterior semblance doth belie
Thy soul's immensity."
WORDSWORTH.

THROUGH the open door the fire-light glowed, and Mary was rocking to and fro and singing a lullaby. This is what she sang :

" Hush-a-bye, Possum, up in the gum ;
The moon is golden, the locusts drum ;
Hush-a-bye, Possum, night comes soon,
When Possums frisk in the light of the moon.

" Hush-a-bye, Blossom, all the day long
The grasses croon you a sleepy song ;
Hush-a-bye, Blossom, soon comes night,
When Fairies dance in the pale moonlight."

The Little Green Road to Fairyland

Robin and Maykin drew softly near, and, on tiptoe, peeped through the window. For they felt something new and strange about the cottage, especially when a green frog hopped out of the door and croaked and croaked at them like a dog barking. Inside Mary was hushing the littlest Baby they had ever seen. Her eyes were shiny as if they were full of moonlight. The children saw at once that Baby was a Fairy.

"What is her name?" asked Maykin, when the song was ended and the Baby laid in her cradle.

"Violet Love," answered Mary. "But I shall call her Fairy, for she *is* a Fairy, you know."

"Yes, I know," Maykin said. "I think it is a lovely name." No one thought anything about the empty cream-jar; Baby was far too exciting, especially when Mary put on her wings and let her fly about a little. The cream-jar was forgotten, too, at Tranquillity Farm, when the children reached home with news of the Fairy Baby. But at bed-time Robin confessed, which was the right thing to do. Mother did not scold, but said she would go next day to see Mary and the Baby, and take another pot of cream.

"Be careful not to fall asleep in the gully!" said Robin. "Gumkin is very greedy." Mother said she would not rest at all in the gully, but Daddy laughed about the Brownies. He was sure the children had dreamt about them and that the cream was accidentally upset in their sleep.

"No! no! no! Daddy!" cried both children.

18

Fairy Days

" Just wait till you *see* Gumkin !   He is coming to see us soon."

Indeed, Gumkin and the other Brownies came that very night while Daddy was sleeping.   In they trooped at the children's open window and perched on their cots, and began to make lovely plans for play in the gully.

Chapter 6

Fairy Days

> " Health that mocks the doctor's rules,
> Knowledge never learned of schools,
> Of the wild-bee's morning chase,
> Of the wild-flower's time and place,
> Flight of fowl and habitude
> Of the tenants of the wood."
>
> J. G. Whittier.

MOST holidays are Fairy days, but how would you like to spend your holidays with a real live Fairy in a fern-gully in the Bush?   Violet Love soon grew into a little girl, but her brown hair had a Fairy shine and curl about it not quite like other children's, and her eyes were like two wild violets, sweet and shy.   She was a sunbeam in Mary's cottage, and like a sunbeam she played in the gully, sometimes alone, and sometimes with Robin and Maykin.

Mary was not very strong now, for she had had a hard and sad life, and she would sit in her rocking-chair for hours stitching little garments for Fairy and dreaming of the Big Man and Lily.   Indeed, I believe she

19

would have gone to them very soon, if it had not been for Fairy.

Sometimes Fairy was allowed to wear her wings for a little while, and fly on them in sunny weather through the golden air. It was a lovely sight, for then her Fairy raiment came back to her, and it seemed as if the tall old gum-trees said " Hush! hush!" and the forest stood quiet to watch. But a Fairy-flight always made Mary a little nervous and anxious; she did not want anyone to know her little girl was a Fairy, and, especially when Fairy made herself tiny with her wand, Mary feared she would fly right away or be gobbled up by a kookaburra. There was not really much danger. The bush creatures soon learnt to know and love Fairy. Wherever she went, Kexy, the frog, hopped after her like a little dog. Kexy was a terrible chatterbox, too, and when he began to croak—as he always did if others began to speak—he drowned all the conversation. The wild violets, of course, were Fairy's dearest friends, and then Robin and Maykin introduced Gumkin and the Brownies to her. Gumkin would do anything for Fairy. His green eyes grew misty with love whenever he looked at her.

Fairy made the dearest, cosiest little home for Mary. You see she was very clever, being a Fairy as well as a little girl. She could bake, and wash, and sweep, and mend ; but Gumkin and his Brownies always came in the mornings to help her with the housework. They were as busy as bees ; some fetched the water, some lit the fire, some set the table, but Gumkin himself always

SOMETIMES FAIRY WAS ALLOWED TO WEAR HER WINGS
FOR A LITTLE WHILE

made toast and superintended. The bustle and chatter ! Often Mary was weak with laughter. It was a merry little home, and anyone would have loved to live there. Fairy knew how to reward the Brownies, for she was a friend of Robin Goodfellow in Fairyland. You all know, of course, that you have only to set out a cream-bowl or saucer of milk at bed-time, and in the night Hobgoblin will do all the work and vanish at cockcrow. Fairy had more cream and milk than she could use from Tranquillity Farm. She was not frightened now of the hens and chickens. It did not startle her if a fluffy yellow ball came cheeping at her out of an egg. But now, you see, she was little-girl size instead of just as tiny as a butterfly.

Robin and Maykin, Fairy and the Brownies, made a lovely little mia-mia in the gully. The roof was a big green tree-fern, the carpet was moss, the chairs were scarlet toadstools, which obligingly shut up when not in use. The beds and curtains were spider-webs, and the plates and cups and pots and pans were gum-nuts and caps. This was a lovely place for picnics; they made a little fire, cooked damper in the glowing embers, and boiled the billy for tea. But the loveliest thing of all was Fairy's eyes. She saw the most wonderful sights with them, and could make Robin and Maykin see too, so that they were just as good as Fairies. Every day there were beautiful new secrets, surprises, and adventures. One of the best of all was the wishing-trees. These were four trees which Fairy brought up by waving her wand; they would spring up from nowhere at the four corners of the mossy space round the mia-mia. One was a cherry-tree, covered with scarlet fruit; one was a red rose bush; one was a singing-bird tree, thick with Fairy birds instead of flowers. I must tell you about the fourth tree. It was a Fairy-tale tree. The Fairy-tales hung thick as apples all over it. They looked like bubbles circling slowly round and round; as you watched, the bubble told you a Fairy-tale, and showed you the pictures, too. If you interrupted, the bubble burst, and you did not hear the end of the story. Sometimes Fairy touched the ground with her wand, and strawberries sprang up everywhere, or great flowers would rise from the moss as big as soup-plates, brimming with milk and honey. There was a dear little plant, too, all made of barley-sugar, with chocolate-creams for fruit.

There was no difficulty about playmates in the gully. Fairy simply called on her flute, and all the bunnies would come frisking, the birds flying, the kangaroos hopping, and even Patsy Possum, who sleeps all day hanging by his tail and frolics all night among the peach-trees, would trot along drowsily rubbing his bright eyes and pink nose. In a pool near the mia-mia lived the Platypus family: Peter, his wife Petronella, and little Peterkin. Fairy and the children loved to swim in the Platypus pool; but they had some very dangerous enemies, too. One of these was the Bunyip, a dreadful old wizard and ogre, who lived in a cave far in the mountains and sometimes sent his willy-willies to whisk people off to the Never-Never. Then there was Koa, chieftain of the Cannibal Imps, who lived 'way back up the creek, sailed in war-canoes, scalped Brownies, and shot people with their poisoned arrows. Koa had blood-red eyes like sparks of flame; he and his Impy-Banditti covered themselves all over with red and yellow and white pipeclay and danced corroborees, and, on purpose, tried to be just as wicked and cruel as they knew how. Another enemy was Lielu the Black Snake with his wife Liena. They lived in the gully and liked to swim in the Platypus pool on hot days. Another thing they loved very much was Platypus eggs, and they had an eye to the two white eggs lying snug in the Platypus burrow. These were the Fairy cradles of Peterkin's little brothers in which they had come from Fairyland. Lielu and Liena would have liked to eat Peter too as well as the eggs, but they feared the poison-spur in his web-footed hind-leg.

Near the pool was Langi-Dorn, the bell-bird's nest, and, on the ferny slope beside the gully, the Lyre-Bird's Bower, all made of twigs and bright with glass beads, parrots' feathers scarlet berries, and shiny shells. Buln-Buln, the lyre-bird, taught them to dance. He was a wonderful mimic, too ; it was great fun to hear him bark like a dog, meow like a pussy-cat, or copy the strokes of the woodman's axe. Other friends were one Leggity Dick, the lame mountain-thrush, who had been caught once in a trap, and the Bluebonnet family, to say nothing of all the Parrots and Cockatoos.

One summer day, sailing boats on the creek,

The Little Green Road to Fairyland

Maykin said, " Where do our little boats go ?" " Down to the great sea !" said Robin. " We have never seen it, but some day Daddy will take us. It is blue as the Kingfisher's wings with white foam like pear-blossom, and great rollers thundering in to the shore."

" Tell us about it, Fairy ?" pleaded Maykin.

So Fairy took her flute and played them music about the great water, and it was like the murmuring of lonely-hearted shells, far inland, for their Mother Sea. She told them too of the mermaids who, on pink-lipped shells, teach the fishes how to sing.

After the song they began to ask what was up the other way, and whence came the silver creek, flowing through its cool green mossy tunnel, and singing on and on to the sea. " Let's go exploring !" they cried. " Some day we will," Fairy promised, " but not yet. I do not know enough yet about Mortal-Land, and there are dangers ahead."

Robin was so glad to hear this; it made him feel all thrilly, throbby, and hop-insidy. He longed more than ever to go exploring. So did Gumkin and his Brownies. Some day they had resolved to march up the gully to war upon Koa and the Cannibal Imps. They were glad it was *Some Day*, but *Some Day* they were determined it should be!

Chapter 7

The School Bell

"They go! they go! I know that they go, but I know not where
they go ;
But I know that they go toward the best—toward something great."
WALT WHITMAN.

HOLIDAYS cannot last for ever. But how should a Fairy know this? What have Fairies to do with lessons or school? On Monday Fairy sat in the gully by the waterfall waiting for her playmates. On Sunday she knew they would not come; for then they followed the calling bells to the little grey church among the gum-trees away down the long high road. Fairy loved the sweet chiming bells each with a prayer in its throat. Some day, when she was big enough, *she* would follow them too; she was too little now to go alone, and Mary was too sick to take her. Fairy did not think of asking anyone else, and besides she was too shy. So Sunday was a lonely day in the gully.

But now it was Monday, and a strange bell was calling, as Fairy waited in the gully. It was not like the wistful Sunday bells all making music together; this was a *cross* bell ; its notes were short, sharp, and stern. They seemed to say, "Quick march! Left, right! Left, right!" as if to soldiers drilling. Fairy ran after the bells, she did not know where or why, and soon she came to the long red road leading to the township. Groups of children were trudging along the road, some

E   25

far ahead and some behind. Their little country boots
clattered sturdily on, and they looked rosy and clean.
Sometimes an old draught-horse would jog along, with
two or three children astride, from the far Bush, or a
pony would canter past with a brisk little rider. The
sun shone, the air sparkled, the blue-gums shed fragrance
all around, magpies warbled from the topmost branches.
All was young and fresh and busy and gay. Most of
the children carried school-bags and lunch-tins, and
Fairy wondered what these were. " I will hide," she
thought, " till they are all ahead, and follow and watch
what happens. I wish I had brought my wings, my
wand, and my flute."

After a while the children turned into a side path
among thick gum-trees and began to climb a hill. The
winding track led into a paddock through slip-rails. The
paddock was thick with deep grass and white daisies. In
the middle was a garden, and among pine-trees a big house
of many windows. Fairy thought it must be a palace.
The bell stopped ringing. A bugle sounded, and all
the children marched into the palace in a procession.
Fairy, who had hidden among the gum-bushes, crept
nearer, and, as no one seemed to notice, she crawled
along the wall under the windows. There was a hum
inside like loud bees. She came to the door; there
was a porch, and hanging on pegs were rows and rows
of little hats, and pink and blue sunbonnets. Fairy
stepped softly through the porch to an inner door.
The door was wide open and she walked in. The
children were sitting at little desks with their backs

SHE BEGAN TO CRY AS IF HER HEART WOULD BREAK

turned away. They could not see Fairy, but they thought a ray of golden sunlight had stolen through the door. The teacher, a tall, neat, frighteningly cross-looking lady, *did* see. She got slowly up, and, as she had such a long neck, Fairy wondered when she would *stop* getting up. Then she pointed a stick at Fairy and said in awful tones, " You are very late, little girl !"

Fairy did not wait to hear any more. She ran faster, faster, for she heard footsteps following behind. Oh, for her fairy wings ! She looked back ; a big boy was following her, but at the slip-rails he stopped and waved to her and laughed. Fairy thought he was shaking his fist. If only she had known it was John, the kind Big Boy, who was afterwards her good friend ! Fairy ran as fast as her little legs would carry her till she came to a grassy patch beside the road. She threw herself down and began to cry as if her heart would break.

Chapter 8

Bruno

" Play up, play up, and play the game !"—NEWBOLT.

"WHY are you crying ?" asked a funny squeaky voice. A wet nose rubbed Fairy's hand, and a furry face snuggled against her cheek. Fairy looked up, and saw the cuddliest brown Baby Bear imaginable. His fists were full of young gum-leaves he had been nibbling, and he put these to Fairy's lips to taste.

27

The Little Green Road to Fairyland

"You darling!" cried Fairy, throwing her two arms round his woolly neck.

"Come, that's better!" said he. "Brighten up, and let's hear the trouble."

"They chased me away from the palace, little brother," said Fairy, "where the children go when the bell rings."

"But they cannot do *that*, little sister!" said the Bear, whose name was Bruno. "The palace is *yours*, and you may go there always! The palace is called School, you know. You ought to have gone long ago! I don't believe you can read or write. I expect the Big Boy was trying to catch you to make you go!"

"Who are they?" asked Fairy.

"That tall lady is the teacher. She is rather a tartar! Those children are the scholars. That Big Boy is clever; he is trying to win a scholarship to college in town."

"Why don't *you* go?" asked Fairy.

"I *am* going," answered Bruno. "I've been too young so far, but Mum and Dad are keen on education, and I'm to get every chance."

"What is education?"

"Oh, it's learning things."

"What things, little Brother?"

"Mostly A, B, C and 1, 2, 3 at first!"

"What for?" asked Fairy, looking puzzled.

"To make you clever, and er—er—successful, and er—er—er—efficient and accomplished, so that you can carve out a career in life. One doesn't know what they *mean*, and they don't *sound* much, but they're the foundation of all true education."

" I see !" said Fairy in a tone of voice as if she did not see at all. " But I should never be brave enough to go."

" It will not do to begin by shirking," said Bruno moralisingly. " You *must* make a start. We *all* have to go *some day*. There's Patsy Possum, Willy Wombat, Hopsy Kangaroo, Wally Wallaby, the Bunny Family, and a score of others all eager for knowledge. *You* make a start. If you report favourably, why, we are all ready to follow. We can all go together, and no one need feel lonesome !"

" But what about me ?" asked poor Fairy.

" Never think of yourself ; it's pure selfishness," said Bruno.

" Do they *hurt* you at school ?" asked Fairy timidly.

" Not if you're a good girl and learn your lessons." Bruno said improvingly : " There's the cane, of course, at times, and some day I shall probably get the cuts myself ; but *you're* only a girl." Bruno strutted about proudly, with a patronising air.

" What are the cuts ?"

" Some one hits you *hard*, *lots* of times, with a stick."

" How *awful*," gasped Fairy, turning pale.

" Well, be good. That's the remedy," Bruno said primly.

" Oh, I will ; at least, I'll try," said poor Fairy. " But when must I go ?"

"To-morrow, when the bell rings," Bruno said
firmly. "You *must* do it for the sake of us all!"

"I will go," said Fairy, her dear little serious face
aglow with love; but she wondered how she would
ever find the courage to face the Tall Lady, the Big
Boy, and all those children. She hugged Bruno hard to
relieve her feelings, then ran to the cottage and helped
Mary to get dinner.

Chapter 9

Fairy Goes to School

"Life is probation, and the earth no goal
But starting point of man."
R. BROWNING.

"MOTHER, when the bell rings to-morrow, may
I go to school?" asked Fairy after dinner.
She was sitting before the fire on a little
stool at Mary's feet.

"Yes, it is time, dear!" said Mary, stroking her
bronzy hair. "I forgot my Fairy was growing such a
big little girl. See that you are clean and tidy, sweetheart. You must always be fresh as a daisy for school,
you know."

"Yes, mother dear," said Fairy, and she kissed
Mary's thin hand and rubbed her little rose-leaf cheek
against it. "Will it be very bad, mother?" asked Fairy
in a lonely voice.

"Nothing can harm you, darling," said Mary, "if
you keep a gentle heart and your soul as white as snow."

30

"YOU *MUST* DO IT FOR THE SAKE OF US ALL!"

Fairy Goes to School

Fairy understood this, and gladly promised to be faithful in all Mary asked.

She did not sleep much that night, for morning was bringing a big, big adventure. Very early, when the golden sun rose in the east, her little friend, One Leggity Dick, woke her, calling at her window with a voice as clear as a bell. "Wake up, wake up, little sister!" carolled Dick.

Fairy was soon as clean and fresh as a daisy; she splashed herself all over till she was white and rosy and dewy with cold sparkling mountain-water. But her frock was very raggity round the hem, though she tried to trim the frayed edges; and it was too short, though she let out all the tucks. She had no socks, and her boots were too small to wear; but Mary brushed her hair till it shone like brown bracken in the sunlight, and Fairy wove a daisy-chain and twisted it round her head, for her old straw hat was shabby and tattered. Mary, whose eyes were dimmed with pain but bright with love, saw nothing wrong with Fairy for her first day at school.

"Come," she called, "I have a brown egg for you, and some toast and tea and honey!"

"*Oh, Mother!*" cried Fairy, running in, "I have let you get breakfast all alone."

"Why, of course, now my big girl must go to school, I can manage very well, and the work is good for me."

Fairy was ready long before the bell began to ring, and Mary stood at the cottage door waving good-bye

31

till she disappeared beyond the gate. Her feet got very dusty as she walked along the red road, and some of the children eyed her curiously. They saw only a little girl in a shabby frock; they could not see the fringe of fairy dew-drops sparkling round the hem. Fairy, though her heart was beating fast, kept her head high and her face steadfastly towards the ringing bell. There was a ferny pool, small and round as the moon, bubbling out of the hillside below the school; in this Fairy washed her feet. "Hello!" said a tiny voice, "Croak! croak! croak! You did not think Kexy would let you come all alone, surely!"

"Sweet, sweet, sweet!" whistled a clear voice from the gum-tree branch above. "You did not think Dick would desert you!"

"See, I have brought my flute, too, and my wand," she said, laughing with joy. "So I am not lonely any more."

Now Fairy walked across the grass among the daisies to keep her feet spotless. Kexy hopped behind and Dicky flew above; and, just to be cheerful, Fairy played a merry tune on the magic flute.

But, oh, dear me! she had not noticed, and all the children were in school, and she was late after all. "You must be brave," she told herself, and marched right into the school, with Kexy and Dick, playing on her flute. The boys and girls gasped with astonishment, and the Tall Lady stared in amazement and indignation. But before she could speak an angry word, the big kind-faced Boy said, "It's the strange little girl, and I

Fairy Goes to School

think she's very frightened." It was only a raggity little girl in a torn frock, with a little rosy face, which was growing whiter and whiter. John rose from his desk and led her gently to the Tall Lady.

" Who are you ?" said she.

" Fairy," answered the little girl.

" Ridiculous !" said the Tall Lady, who was also called the Duchess. " I mean, what is your name, and where do you come from ?"

" Fairy, from Fairyland !"

The class laughed; they could not see a Fairy— not yet—only a shabby Bush child. But the Tall Lady rapped on her desk for silence, and looked sternly at the children.

"Of course, you are not telling the truth, and I shall call you Mary."

" True as true, I *am* a Fairy !" said poor little Fairy, choking back the tears.

" Do not try to be funny !" the Teacher said, " and take off that silly wreath !" She snatched off the daisy crown and tossed it into the waste-paper basket. " School is *very* bad !" Fairy said to herself. " But you must be brave and keep a gentle heart." For she was beginning to feel a little angry as well as unhappy. " She is stubborn and stupid !" the Tall Lady said. " John, take her to the Infant Room."

John smiled kindly at Fairy as he took her hand and gave it a tiny squeeze, and into the other one he put a big rosy apple. Fairy began to love John, and she smiled at him through her tears.

The Infant Room was much better. Robin and Maykin were there, and there were pictures on the wall, and fresh flowers and pot-plants, and the Teacher was like a lovely Princess out of a story, the golden-haired, blue-eyed sort, that always marries a Fairy Prince.

Chapter 10

The First Day at School

"For the good are always the merry,
Save by an evil chance,
And the merry love the fiddle,
And the merry love to dance."
W. B. YEATS.

"I'VE brought you a Fairy!" said John, smiling at the Princess. A hush fell over the room, and the Princess opened her arms. Fairy ran right into them. "So you are a Fairy!" said the Princess.

"True as true!" said Fairy, gulping back the tears. "Why, children," cried the Princess, "a real live Fairy has come to school with us! Now all sorts of lovely things will happen!"

"She *is* a Fairy!" said Robin, while Maykin nodded her head eagerly. "We've known her since she came from Fairyland, and she has lovely wings at home, and she can fly with them."

"Yes, and a Fairy wand and flute," said Maykin. "Some day she will fly away to Fairyland."

The children's eyes sparkled; some of the little ones in the Infant Room could see that she was a Fairy,

The First Day at School

and noticed the sparkly fringe round her frayed frock. One little girl saw only the torn edge and the bare feet. But she knew Fairy was very pretty.

" Is she Cinderella ?" she asked.

" Why, no, Cinderella went off long ago," said another, " to the Fairy Prince's Palace."

" And some day you will ride away with Prince Charming," said the Fairy, looking earnestly at the Princess.

Her soft cheeks grew pinker, but she laughed, and said to the children, " You must be very loving and kind to our Fairy, or she will fly away before the Fairy things happen !" " Yes, yes !" all the children shouted joyously, and Robin and Maykin made room between them for Fairy, and Robin fetched her a tiny chair. They were all sitting round a table making boats and dolls and flowers with coloured paper. Fairy began to feel as if she would like school very much. " Fairy will tell us about Fairyland," said the Princess, putting her arm round Fairy and kissing her, " and we will tell her about mortal-land. Wouldn't that be nice, sweetheart ?"

Fairy felt quite happy now; her heart overflowed with love and gratitude. She longed to do something big and splendid for the Princess.

The Princess was really the loveliest teacher a child ever had ! In playtime she turned the skipping rope, or joined in Tiggy or ring-a-rosy; but this day Fairy told stories instead.

But, alas and alas for Kexy and Dicky ! Fairy did not know it, but some of the Big Boys had caught

35

them both, and meant to keep them for school pets. Poor little Dicky was imprisoned in a wire cage, and poor little Kexy in a wooden box. True, there was clear fresh water in the cage, and scraps of food, and green grass and leaves in the box, and plenty of fat flies. But oh, dear, dear! it was terrible! And Dick and Kexy did not know how to tell Fairy. The silly little things forgot that Boys cannot understand Fairy Talk; so they just drooped and moped in their little prisons.

Before school closed for the day, the Tall Lady sent for Fairy, and told her she must have a tidy frock and some shoes and stockings by to-morrow. How to do it Fairy could not guess; Mary was too ill to make a new frock in time, and Fairy could not make a mortal frock, though a Fairy one would have been easy.

At the end of school, the Princess said:

"Do you like school, Fairy? Will you come to-morrow?"

"I have no frock or boots!"

"Why, Fairy," said the Princess, "just *wish* for them and see if a mortal-wish can come true as well as a fairy-wish! In the morning look in the bread-box, and you will find the mortal frock and shoes." Then she asked her this, "Have you any little friends away back in the Bush?"

"Oh, yes, ever so many!"

"And wouldn't *they* like to come to school too?"

"Yes, but they're too scared!"

"Oh, the little shy ones! But what made *you* come, Fairy?"

"I came for the others, to try it!"

"Do you like it, Fairy?"

"I do, if *you* are here!" said Fairy.

"Oh, Fairy," said the Princess, hugging her, "bring the others *soon!*"

"Soon as we can patch them up a bit," Fairy promised, nodding and smiling. "They're rather rough, and haven't very good manners."

"Bring them along!" the Princess said. "We shall love them all, if they are like *you!*" But she said the last part to herself, for she did not want to spoil Fairy. So Fairy scampered off after the other children, as the Princess waved good-bye.

But poor little Dicky and Kexy were left behind at school. If only Dicky had had the sense to whistle or Kexy to croak Fairy would have heard; but they were both too miserable, and it made them a little dull and foolish.

Chapter 11

Lielu, the Black Snake

"And there, they say, two bright and agèd Snakes

Bask in the glens."

M. ARNOLD.

SOME of the rougher, ruder school-children were waiting round the gate as Fairy ran out. They began to sing:

"Fairy, Fairy, all forlorn,
Dressed like a scarecrow, tattered and torn."

37

The Little Green Road to Fairyland

Fairy was terribly hurt. "I could make you all vanish with my wand," she said, "but instead I will keep a gentle heart." This made the children laugh and shout louder than ever. They had never heard anything like it before, and they began to pepper Fairy's little bare legs with pea-shooters. But John had stayed behind the rest to do some extra work for his scholarship; when he came by, the rough ones scattered, and John escorted Fairy along the road safely till she caught up with Robin and Maykin, who were walking slowly on purpose. Then John turned into a Bush-track that led another way, but the unkind children followed Fairy behind at a distance, and sometimes faintly Fairy could hear "tattered and torn" and "all forlorn."

It was a very hot day. The children were glad to reach a bend in the road, where there was soft green grass, and the creek flowed into quiet pools among the ferns. Here the children rested, and took off socks and shoes to paddle in the cool water. Soon the unkind children caught up, and they too waded in the creek, and forgot to tease Fairy. Humpy, one of the boys who had been cruellest, was sitting astride a log, dipping his feet into the water. He did not see Lielu, the Black Snake, gliding up, with his wife Liena close beside. Suddenly Lielu darted at him, and wound himself round one bare leg; then he reared up his neck and stared at Humpy with his wicked eyes, flicking his tongue in and out like a flame. "I can kill you if I wish!" he hissed. "You know I can.

38

Lielu, the Black Snake

Move, and I will! Do not move, and I will! You cannot escape! You dug up all our eggs, and killed our baby-snakes! Now I will kill *you!* S-s-s-s-s!" There seemed no way to save Humpy. He sat paralysed. He knew, like all Bush-children, it was death to move. The others stood spellbound and speechless with horror.

Then Fairy took from her pocket her little silver flute. She played the merry locust-tune, and the cool water-tune, the spring song of nesting bluebonnets, and the sunshine song that wakens snakes from winter sleep. So the silver flute ran on.

Lielu gradually unwound his coils from Humpy's leg, slid along the log, and swayed on his tail from side to side in time to Fairy's fluting. "So away home—home—home!" sang the silver flute. "Home, and sleep—sleep—sleep!" As Fairy piped and Lielu danced, little by little she drew away from the children towards the thick bracken. At last she blew two or three harsh notes on the flute, and Lielu darted into a hollow log and vanished, with his wife Liena close behind. "Revenge—revenge!" they hissed.

"No," said Fairy, "for the great grey Kookaburra will gobble you up—up—up. Hark how he laughs!" And a chorus of elfin laughter broke from the top of the tall white river-gum. The circle of watching children stood white-faced and astonished at first, but Humpy walked up to Fairy and shook hands. "I'm sorry," he said gruffly. "I *do* believe you're a Fairy, and—and—anyhow you're a sport!" And Fairy just smiled and said nothing, But her heart was happy. She knew she had won another friend in freckle-faced Humpy. And now quite a number of the school-children knew she was a really truly Fairy.

Chapter 12

The Mortal Frock

" What forms are these coming
So white through the gloom ?"
M. ARNOLD.

HOW glad Mary was to welcome home her Fairy child and to hear the news of the first day at school! But Fairy just told the happy parts, for Mary looked very frail and thin, and was too ill to be worried. So she told about the Princess, and the Big Boy's rosy apple, and Robin and Maykin ; but she said nothing of her torn frock, the teasing boys, and Lielu, the Black Snake.

" May I wear my Fairy wings to school some day, Mother dear ?" she coaxed. " The Princess and the children would love them, and the Tall Lady would believe that I am a Fairy."

" Do not fly away from me, then," said Mary.

" Never, never!" promised Fairy earnestly, " not till you go to Lily and the Big Man ! But I will wait till the Bush Boys go to school, and wear my wings that day for a surprise." But Fairy had to wear her wings sooner than that day. As she was sleeping in the moonlight, a little green figure stole through the

40

window, perched on her pillow, and gently pulled one of her curls. He was sniffing and sobbing, and big tears were rolling slowly down his cheeks!

"Whatever is wrong, Gumkin dear?" whispered Fairy, sitting up in bed.

"It's D-D-Dicky and K-K-Kexy!" sobbed Gumkin. "They're in c-c-cages at school, and, boo-hoo-oo, Lielu and Liena are going to kill and eat them at d-d-dawn to pay you out. Oh, poor little froggy and birdy!" He put his fists in his eyes and howled dismally.

"Sh!" said Fairy, "stop crying and *do* something. You hold these till I come!" She gave him the wand and flute, and, opening the cupboard, shook out the fairy wings and fastened them to her shoulders. Then she flew through the window, with Gumkin close behind, and did not pause a minute until she reached the school-house on the hill.

It seemed to be all locked up, but a light glimmered in a little room at the back, and Fairy saw the Tall Lady correcting exercises with a blue pencil.

"Kexy and Dicky are in the big schoolroom!" whispered Gumkin. "How shall we get to them!"

"Croak! croak! Cheep! cheep!" two sorrowful voices called from the big schoolroom. "Quick! quick! Save us!" Fairy and Gumkin were so upset to hear this, that they forgot all about the Tall Lady, and flew right over her table and her lamp, from the little room into the big schoolroom. Fairy flew to Dick and Gumkin to Kexy, and, in a moment, unfastening their prison-doors, took up the shivering little creatures, and hugged them in their loving arms.

"What is the meaning of all this?" said a terrible voice. The Tall Lady stood in the schoolroom with her lamp raised high and a black frown on her face. "Take, oh, take that face away!" screamed Gumkin, and, in a reckless agony of terror, he touched himself on the heart with the top of the magic wand, and suddenly vanished right out of sight. Kexy was left, for the magic wand had not touched *him*. He hopped into Fairy's arms, and with Dick in one and Kexy in the other, she stood facing the Tall Lady and smiling bravely. "We came to save them," she explained, "from Lielu, the Black Snake. I am sorry if we startled you. Good-night." Fairy flew over the Tall Lady's head, out of the open door, and home.

The Tall Lady walked into the little room, and set down the lamp on the table. "Dear me!" she said, "what a strange dream! It must be that queer child from the Bush! Or else it's those tiresome exercises! I'll just look if the Bird and Frog are safe." She looked; Dicky's cage was empty; Kexy's box was empty; the Bird and the Frog were gone!

Meanwhile Fairy had reached home safely. She had folded her wings away, put Dicky and Kexy to bed, and she was fast asleep herself. Little did she dream that poor Gumkin was *nowhere*. You see, he had put himself out, like a popped bubble, with the magic wand. Like a little silly he remembered to touch his *heart* with the *top* of the wand for vanishing, and forgot what he must do to come back again. This is what he should have done : touched his *nose* with the *tip* of the magic wand. Once you disappear it is the only way to reappear. The Brownies sat on toad-stools all night long and wailed for Gumkin in the moonlight; but he never came home. Do not feel too despondent about him, however, little Brownies! There is no doubt Gumkin is in peril; in fact, worse than that, Gumkin is *nowhere* at all. But, after all, there is Fairy, and she loves Gumkin dearly.

How happy Fairy felt in the sunshiny morning! Dicky was singing at the window and Kexy was croaking at the door. She ran to the gate and peeped into the bread-box. There was a great big parcel. "Mother, mother! Look!" called Fairy, and together they opened it. Inside was a little pink frock, a sun-bonnet, white socks, and little black slippers; the promise of the Princess had come true!

Chapter 13

Lost, Stolen, or Strayed—a Frog, a Bird, and a Little Brown-ee!

"A total and absolute blank."—LEWIS CARROLL.

FAIRY looked so sweet when she arrived at school next morning in her pink frock, that even the Tall Lady smiled at her. She thought her adventure of the night before was all a dream. But at roll-call one of the Big Boys raised his hand

and said, "The thrush and frog are gone!" The
Tall Lady was exceedingly angry, and asked, in blood-
curdling tones, who had had the audacity to enter the
school precincts out of hours and interfere with school
property. Fairy did not understand all the long
words, but she could guess what was wrong.

"I did!" she said, and her cheeks grew pink.
"You *know* I did. You saw me. I flew in on my
wings last night and let them go. Besides they are
mine, and *ought* to be free. It is very cruel to cage
our little wild Brothers!" Fairy's cheeks were like
twin red roses and her eyes like stars. She even
stamped her foot; but a Fairy's foot would not make
much sound, however hard she stamped.

"No, she didn't!" said freckled Humpy, rising in
his place. "*I* did it." Now this was not true; but
Humpy wanted to save Fairy from punishment, because
she had rescued him from Lielu. Besides she was
such a dear little girl, and now all the Boys wanted to
help her.

"Oh, what a wicked story!" squeaked a shrill
voice in the air. "Me and her did it together last
night. We burgled in and scared the Duchess; but
we let Dick and Kexy go. Tra-la-la! Tra-la-la!
Tra-la-la! Catch me, if you can!" I need hardly
tell you it was Gumkin, who had blown himself out
like a bubble. "Who is speaking?" asked the Tall
Lady. "Tell me at once."

"It's me! Now I'm here, now I'm there. Now
I'm sitting on the Duchess' hair!" carolled Gumkin,

SHE FLEW THROUGH THE WINDOW, WITH
GUMKIN CLOSE BEHIND.

merry as a cricket; and he did perch on the Tall Lady's hair. Really puzzled, she put up both hands to catch him, but now the shrill voice piped all over the room, and they could hear something fluttering about like a bat. "You can't cane me, because I'm *nowhere!*" laughed Gumkin, as he saw the Tall Lady preparing to get her cane. It was very funny to see the Tall Lady holding a conversation with the empty air, as it seemed. She kept turning her head this way and that to answer Gumkin's remarks, as he flapped briskly to and fro.

"I can at least cane *some one*," she said sternly.

"I do not know which is guilty, Mary or Humphrey, but I can very well imagine you are equally to blame. Stand forward!" Then a wonderful thing happened. The night before Gumkin had hidden the Fairy wand in a cupboard. There was a creak, and the cupboard door slowly opened; out came the wand, and all by itself, they thought (for no one could see Gumkin), it shot like an arrow at the Tall Lady and its shining top stood against her heart. Like a flash of lightning she was gone and the cane after her. Wouldn't that be fun in school? You can just guess how the children jumped and laughed and clapped. Kexy came croaking in too, and Dicky sang on the window-sill. Then Fairy seized the magic wand, which was floating about in the air, and said: "Come here, Gumkin. Take the wand and touch your nose with the tip." "Deeds, not words!" cried Gumkin, and turning two somersaults, he stood before them on the teacher's desk, bowed low, and doffed his cap, and laid his hand on his heart. "Where is she?" asked the children, when they could speak for laughing.

"Nowhere!" said Gumkin. "The cane's nowhere for evermore, but how long the Duchess will be nowhere depends on Fairy's pleasure."

Then he flew through the door, crying "Cheerio!"

A swarm of mournful Brownies had been lurking near, for they knew Gumkin was lost in the schoolhouse. When he appeared, with triumphant squeaks they lifted him shoulder-high, and bore him off to his mossy home in the creek.

Of course all these events were rather surprising. But everyone was getting used to surprises since Fairy came to school. This day John had to teach the bigger children, and they thought he was a splendid school-master. The Princess, of course, looked after the little ones. In the middle of lessons Kexy and Dick marched in arm-in-arm, and, in a brief speech, explained that they were willing to be the school-pets-in-chief, provided they were free and not caged. It was just the place for Kexy; he was such a chatterbox and so argumentative, while Dicky was a great help on singing-days.

Fairy had now recovered her magic wand. With its help she soon turned the school-grounds into a fairy garden of loveliness. All the sweet flowers that had blossomed and gone in the past she called back again, all the flowers little children had loved in that school in vanished days—violets, primroses and mignonette, pansies, roses and lilies—and she starred the school paddock with wild-flowers knee-deep, so that their fragrance was carried on the wind for miles around. Humpy watered the garden faithfully; on the hottest days he never failed; and at night the Fairies came with their little watering-cans of dew-drops. One day in playtime, at ring-a-rosy, a lovely thing happened: Fairy touched the grass in the heart of the circle with her wand, and up sprang a little cherry-tree thick with ripe red cherries.

Another day she tapped the ground quickly here, there, and everywhere, and wherever the wand touched the earth, ripe scarlet wild-strawberries grew.

And all this time the Tall Lady was away, and John began to look thin and worried; for, though she was so stern, no one could help him in his scholarship work like the Tall Lady. Now too the Princess told Fairy it was time to bring her little friends to school. "On Monday, then," Fairy promised. "That will give us Saturday for tubs and tidying."

So Fairy said they would come on Monday for certain sure.

"I wish we had the Duchess back," said the Princess. "We shall need her help with so many new scholars. Besides, John will lose his scholarship, unless she come soon." "Oh, is it too late?" said Fairy in anguish. "Perhaps not," but soon it will be." Fairy had never seen the Princess look so grave.

" I will have her here to-morrow with my wand," she said. The Princess smiled, but Fairy sped away to Gumkin's nest (for Brownies live in nests of moss on the tip-top of gum-trees) and sent him off with the wand to discover and bring home the Duchess. It was very, very unselfish, but she did it for John.

Chapter 14

The Bush Boys get Ready for School

"To-morrow, dearest Piso, one will come
To lead thee to a philosophic home."
GREEK ANTHOLOGY.

YOU will not be surprised to hear that Mary's cabin was all ablossom with flowers. A red rose-bush stood at one side of the door, and a white rose-bush at the other ; the borders were thick with violets, and Lily's little green hillock never missed a tall white lily. Mary was quite excited about the Bush Boys at school. She said she would help with the mending, but her hands were too weak to do much. After tea Fairy wrote a letter to Bruno on a big blue-gum-leaf. Her pen was a rosella feather and her ink wild-raspberry juice. It was Fairy writing, quite different from mortal, and the letter said this :

" DARLINGEST BUSH BOYS,
" Please meet us on Saturday morning under the Big Tree-Fern near the mia-mia. Business : Washing,

48

THE BUSH BOYS WERE A GREAT SUCCESS AT THE PARTY.

The Bush Boys get Ready for School

mending, tidying! Bring your clothes. Important. Good-bye, little Brothers. Love and kisses, from FAIRY.

"x x x—o o o—x x x—o o o—x x x—o o o."

All the Boys gathered under the tree-fern in good time on Saturday morning. Robin brought soap and a scrubbing brush from the farm for washing, and Maykin her little work-basket for mending. Fairy had engaged two hundred spiders to help. Bruno was there, of course, with his Baby Brother, Gumkin and the Brownies, Patsy Possum, Hopsy Kangaroo, Peterkin Platypus, the big Bunny family, and the little Kookaburras.

They brought such funny clothes! Most of them grew on their skins, and Maykin was very much afraid she would hurt when mending patches in their fur, or trimming the rough edges of feathers. Robin set to work busily with the washing, helped by Gumkin and Bruno. They washed in the Platypus Pool, and Peterkin's Dad was quite annoyed because he got soap in his eye. Meanwhile Fairy and Maykin fitted on new suits and mended old ones. Some of the clothes needed a great deal of mending. Bruno had worn out his only corduroy pants with climbing so many gum-trees. He had to have a big tartan patch on them, for it was the only material Maykin had large enough. But Bruno thought it very pretty and was highly delighted. He felt that he was one of the Gay Gordons, as he strutted about humming, "The Campbells are Coming," or striking attitudes, and reciting " Young Lochinvar !" " I will buy a glengarry to match," he said. So, just to humour him, Fairy made a little glengarry, which he cocked on one side of his head in a rakish way. Polly Rosella, the only girl amongst the new scholars, was very vain. She considered her bright gown of feathers becoming and stylish. " I shall be the belle of the school," she simpered, as she fanned herself with her wing.

" Yes, it is a very pretty frock," said Fairy, " but I hope it will not be thought too bright."

In the end, with very hard work, all were ready. The big Bunny family had clean white collars and neat neckties, and the Kookaburras a row of pale blue buttons down their brown jackets.

Joey Cockatoo's yellow crest was a little perky. But after all it was only telling the truth, for he was a cheeky bird. Then Robin explained the school-rules as well as he could. He did not really understand them properly himself. " It's best not to talk at *all* at first," he said. " If you say nothing, you know, you say nothing wrong." This sounded reasonable, but Polly and Joey looked droopy. They were chatterboxes, and loved to talk.

" You must stay where they put you and never *hop* in school," he told Hopsy and Wally.

" Is that down in black and white ?" asked Hopsy.

" Well, no, but hopping in school isn't *done*."

" It's time it began then," said Hopsy, " if they

want kangaroos at school! How else are we to get about?"

Robin could not say, so he hastily changed the subject by addressing the birds. "You birds must never sing in class. You had better chirp, and Patsy Possum mustn't sleep. It's not respectful. Then, Gumkin, *you* must be careful. Your manners are *shocking!* At least the Duchess would think so!" he added hastily, for Gumkin was looking rather offended. "Bruno, you must not climb in school, or eat gum-nuts, or chew wattle-gum. And Buln-Buln, you must never mimic the teacher. Bell-bird, you must not ring too early. Georgy Goanna, you must not poke out your tongue in school, even to catch flies. That would be *awful*. Dear me! you will have to be careful," said Robin, looking anxious.

"Of course, if the worst comes to the worst I can always make them vanish with the wand, or else the Duchess," Fairy said reassuringly. And everyone thought this a great comfort. "All be ready to march to school early on Monday morning," said Fairy. "See that your fur is well combed and your claws scrubbed!" The Bush Boys promised, and all went home to their burrows and nests well pleased with their neat clothes.

Chapter 15

The Bush Boys at School

"Ha! I see!
Doris has made a prisoner of thee;
And now instructs thee by thy proper smart
How very mischievous a thing thou art."
GREEK ANTHOLOGY.

NO one was late on Monday morning. School was too exciting an adventure to miss. There was a great fuss and fluster in the nests and burrows and pools and trees, as the Mummies and Daddies woke and got the children ready for school. The little Bunnies took a long time to comb; there were so many of them. The little Kookaburras *would* laugh, as if everything was one big joke. Even Gran'dad Kookaburra, a wise old grey head, could not persuade them to be serious. The Brownies polished up their buttons, and smoothed the feathers in their caps, and did their utmost to wear a sedate expression. As it was, Patsy Possum nearly kept them late. He *would not* wake up. Possums, you know, hunt all night and sleep all day; and Patsy had been in the peach-trees at Tranquillity Farm. But at last he rubbed his sharp pink nose, uncurled his ring-tail, stretched and yawned, and crawled reluctantly out of bed.

52

HE HAD TO HAVE A BIG TARTAN PATCH ON THEM

The Bush Boys at School

Soon the procession was ready. First came Fairy with her wings and magic flute; behind her Robin and Maykin carried the Union Jack and the Southern Cross; the others followed, like Noah's Ark, two and two, keeping perfect time. It would seem hard to us for such assorted creatures to march in good order; but they were Fairy things, and followed Fairy piping. As they wound along over the school paddock all the children ran to watch. Just imagine a Fairy flying on wings to *your* school, and all those fluffy furry creatures following. It is not polite or kind to stare at new scholars, but the children were hardly to blame this time.

The Duchess had come back from nowhere, fetched by Gumkin. I am afraid he gave her nose rather a sharp tap with the tip of the wand, but anyway he made her visible. She was becoming used by this time to surprises and shocks; this made the arrival of the Bush Boys less amazing than you would have expected. The Princess got a great surprise; she thought Fairy's little friends would be Bush children from the forest; not all those Brownies, Beasties, and Birds. It was difficult to squeeze them all in, but somehow they managed it, for where there's a will, there's a way.

From the first minute it was clear the Boys would be in constant scrapes. They simply *could not* keep the rules. The Duchess loved the Baby Kookaburras straightaway, because they always laughed at her jokes, which no other scholar seemed to see. Everything

53

the Duchess said made the Kookaburras chuckle, and this charmed her, for she had not been considered amusing before.

The Bush Boys were *awful*. They would all talk together. They shouted out the answers to questions all together, and all in different speech! no one could hear if anyone was right, and no one could be sure if anyone was wrong. The din was deafening. The Boys got so excited; Polly and Joey *would* screech; Hopsy and Wally skipped up and down; the Baby Kookaburras roared with laughter, and Bruno stood on his head, and shouted "Hurroosha!" This made the whole school laugh; his tartan patch was so funny, and Winky, the smallest and naughtiest of the Brownies, shot a paper dart at it. Winky had to confess, and he was put on the Dunce's stool, with a Dunce's cap on his head.

Fairy thought he had been unkind to Bruno, so at first she did nothing. But when she saw big tears slowly coming down Winky's face, she waved her wand, the cap flew out of the window, and the stool just vanished, and Winky sat on the floor with a thud and cried harder than ever. Fairy had forgotten he would have nothing to sit on when the stool disappeared.

Winky was much the worst child at school. He got his name because he was always winking one of his big green eyes. He said he could not help it; he came from Fairyland that way. They could do nothing with Willy Wagtail, for he was continually

The Bush Boys at School

" wagging it." Georgy Goanna often got into trouble for putting his tongue out to catch flies, and the Lyre-Bird, Buln-Buln, was kept in for mimicking the Duchess. He had to write out ever so many lines about politeness and good manners ; but instead he wrote " Imitation is the sincerest flattery." This rather pleased the Duchess ; she was kinder to Buln-Buln ever after. It was a little awkward for her having no cane, no Dunce's cap, no Dunce's stool ; she had not even a corner in which to put the little children, for Fairy had made the corners vanish, and there simply were no corners. And if you ask me how I account for this, I don't account for it at all. I simply state the facts, and remind you that a Fairy can do anything. All this time we have forgotten Fairy and her lustrous wings. Do you know that the Duchess and some of the children could not even see them, nor the little wreath of flowers round her brow ? But the Princess saw, and John, and all the littlest children. She flew round and round the schoolroom for them, and let them touch and stroke her shimmery feathers ; she even allowed them to fly a little, but the Princess feared the wings would be broken, and all the children could do was to flutter a little near the ground.

I forgot to say that Bruno was wonderful at arithmetic. He could figure a sum out better than the book, and he gave much more interesting answers. For instance, he was much quicker than anyone in the class to get results like this :

(a)	3 eggs	...	...	...	4½d.		(b)	2 apples
	1 lb. flour		...	...	3½d.			10 grapes
	½ lb. butter		...	...	2d.			1 pear
	½ lb. raisins		...	...	4½d.			6 oranges
	½ glass milk		...	...	1d.			2 bananas
	¾ lb. sugar		...	...	3d.			20 peanuts

<table>
<tr><td>Result : Cakes.</td><td>Result : Fruit.</td></tr>
</table>

Why, all the rest expressed the answer in dull old money or numbers.

Chapter 16

Jasper, the Little Musician

"Heard melodies are sweet, but those unheard
Are sweeter ; therefore, ye soft pipes, play on."

KEATS.

ONE day, when school was dismissed, Fairy ran back to get her spelling book, which she had forgotten. The Duchess was sitting at her desk with her head on her hands crying. Fairy had never seen a grown-up cry, and of all people, the Duchess! She could scarcely believe what she saw, but her wise little heart told her what to do. She just climbed on her knee, put both her arms round her neck, and hugged hard. She knew she would soon hear all the trouble.

"Why are you so sad?" she whispered after a while.

"My little brother is lame."

"I am sorry," said Fairy.

Jasper, the Little Musician

" He is a little musician !"

" That is lovely. Does not that make him happy ?"

" No ; for he cannot play the music of his heart's desire, and without it he will die."

" May I see him ?" asked Fairy. " What is his name, and where does he live ?"

" He lives in the great city, in a hospital, and I think it would make you sorrowful to see him."

" Why, no !" said Fairy. " I will help him ! Will you bring him here to the sweet wild country ? Say yes, please, say yes ! I will teach him to play the music of his heart's desire, and he will live, and forget that he is lame. I can, you know, for I am a Fairy," she said gravely, nodding her head.

" I believe you are !" said the Duchess, kissing her, and she smiled and sighed both together. " Well, I will get little Jasper here for a time, and see if he improves in health." At that moment the Duchess looked at the child, and caught a flash of shimmering jewels round the fringe of her frock, and a crown of more than earthly flowers round her hair. But, feeling that she was becoming too sentimental, she gave herself a shake, and said to Fairy more gruffly than she meant : " Run along home now, Fairy ! Your mother will be anxious."

But Fairy knew the Duchess was beginning to love her, because it was the very first time she had called her Fairy instead of Mary.

A few days after this Jasper arrived. He was a little cripple, with a gentle, sad face, and he looked very frail and delicate. He made friends with Fairy at once.

"Why are you so sad?" asked Fairy, as they wandered together among the daisies of the school paddock. "Is it *this?*" she touched his leg gently.

"It is more the music I cannot play. I should forget *this* if I could get the music right."

"Play to me," said Fairy; "we will rest here, and you shall have my little flute." So they sat down and Jasper put the Fairy flute to his lips. But no sooner had he began to play—at first stammeringly—than the full round notes came gushing out like golden bubbles, bubble on bubble, and the pink came into Jasper's pale face, and his eyes sparkled. Then the notes soared up, up, up into the blue like a skylark's song, and the music hung tremulous in space a little; then down, down, down it floated, and at last sank quivering into the flute again. Then Jasper played a little wild woodland melody. You could hear the elves tripping, and the bunnies frisking in the moonlight, bats cheeping, and the little owl hooting to his mate across the dark forest pool. Then came goblins marching two and two; a little witch whizzed on a broomstick over the sky, and a little child who had followed her was lost in the tangled wood, and cried for his mother. Will o' the Wisp was leading him into the miry swamp, when a Shining One stood on the margin and scattered stars all along his way, and he followed the starry guides safe home to his mother's arms. There you heard the child's laugh, and the

THEN JASPER PLAYED A LITTLE WILD WOODLAND MELODY

mother's voice of love, and her lullaby as she rocked the child to sleep.

" It is the music, the music I have dreamed of so long !" cried Jasper, throwing down the flute and trying to dance in spite of his lame leg. " It has come to me !" He almost wept for joy. " But I have never played like that before, and never can again without the wonder-flute."

" It is yours !" said Fairy, putting it into his hands. " Keep it always, and some day you will be a great musician. You will play before the King and the Queen on their golden thrones, and the poor and sick will rejoice at the Fairy piping."

Jasper laughed happily and wrapped the Fairy flute in his crimson silk scarf, and hugged it in his arms with love. Now his cheeks began to grow so round and red, and his little face was so bright, that the Duchess grew joyful too. In these days the school was a very happy place ; red roses climbed riotously over it ; John won his scholarship and went away to a big school in the city ; Prince Charming came on his milk-white charger and carried off the Princess. Gran'dad Kookaburra ate up Lielu, Liena, and all their little ones. Now, instead of that cross-patch bell, the Bell-bird sat on the school turret every morning to call the children to school.

Chapter 17

Sylvie's Frock

"Then to Sylvia let us sing,
    That Sylvia is excelling ;
She excels each mortal thing
    Upon the dull earth dwelling :
To her let us garlands bring."

SHAKESPEARE.

FAIRY went and sat among the wild violets and cried a little when Jasper had taken away her Fairy flute. The fragrance of the violets was all around her like love, and she thought : "He needs it more than I. Now he can always play the Music of Heart's Desire." Kexy and Dicky sat one on each shoulder as she cried, and wiped away the big falling tears as they rolled down, until Fairy had to laugh. She got up, and danced along through the forest, with Dicky flying above and Kexy hopping before. There was wild heath out all through the Bush, crimson, pink, and white, and in a mossy space among it Fairy found a little girl weeping bitterly. It was Sylvie, the charcoal-burner's little daughter. The charcoal-burner was very poor ; his wife and baby had died of want ; little Sylvie was thin and frail, but her yellow hair was like the daffodils of spring, and her blue eyes like the bluebells.

"Oh, tell me what is wrong," said Fairy, sitting down beside her. "You can't do anything !" said Sylvie. "You are just as poor yourself."

60

Sylvie's Frock

"But what more could we do, if we were not poor?"

"We could buy beautiful frocks for the Rich Little Girl's party in the Big House."

"Oh, yes, I remember!" said Fairy. "She has asked us all to her Birthday Party on Saturday. How lovely!"

"But I cannot go," said Sylvie sorrowfully, "for I have only this!" And she held out the skirt of her shabby spotted cotton frock.

"It would not quite do for a party, I suppose," Fairy said pensively, "although you make it look very pretty on you. But wait; *I* know!"

Mary's cottage was not far off, and Fairy just flew to it, opened the cupboard, and in a few minutes ran back with her beautiful Fairy wings and her little work-basket.

"But you are not going to cut up *those!*" cried Sylvie in horror. They were soft and shimmering pale violet, like the sky at twilight, but the tissue of Fairy wings is of unearthly beauty. Fairy, as she looked at them, felt her mortal heart leap and throb, and in case her courage should fail, she quickly made a big cut in the right wing, so that it was spoilt for flying; now it was too late to change her mind. Such a fitting and cutting there was, as they shaped the wings into a lovely little frock for Sylvie! Then out from the heath came hundreds of spiders, and just in a few minutes they sewed the frock with such tiny stitches as were invisible.

The Little Green Road to Fairyland

Sylvie looked radiant in the frock—more like a flower than a child. But no wonder, when it was made of the stuff of Fairy wings. At the party Sylvie's beauty astonished everyone, and the mothers were all talking about the frock, and wondering how the charcoal-burner could afford it. "It would be more sensible to give the child good food," they said. How they smiled when Sylvie said her frock was made of Fairy wings ; but, later on, they believed ; for, when they asked Fairy to let them see her fly, she could not fly. She had no Fairy wings any more. "And how shall I get home to Fairyland?" she thought to herself. "For, even suppose I find my Fairy heart and the golden key, how shall I fly across the space between here and there with no wings?" But of course she was happier because of Sylvie than sad because of herself.

The Bush Boys were a great success at the party ; every one came, Jasper too with his Fairy flute. Winky disgraced himself by shutting one eye repeatedly at the Rich Little Girl's Great-Aunt Priscilla, who was a bit proper. The Rich Little Girl thought this very funny. Then Bruno, who had come in his glengarry and a tartan tie, did the Highland Fling all alone on the ballroom dais. Fairy was ashamed of their table-manners at supper, but Gumkin and the Brownies made graceful waiters, in spite of a few accidents, such as squirting lemonade into Great-Aunt Priscilla's eye, and dropping hot soup or ice-cream down folks' collars. At supper a squabble arose between Bruno and Winky as to which had eaten the most supper. They became so furious that they pelted each other with ice-cream and jellies, grabbing it from the table in handfuls like mud, and flinging it at each other. For Bruno said he was bigger, and could hold more; and Winky said he was quicker, and made things disappear more rapidly. The only thing to do was to make them vanish with the magic wand; but the fight went on for a while, and after that chattering and squealing could be heard in the air; jellies and ice-creams continued to fly; though no one could see who threw them. Of course, the fight was a pity, but it was a good idea in a way. The Rich Little Girl was delighted, and, after all, it was *her* party. A black-currant-jam tart struck Great-Aunt Priscilla right on the tip of her nose, which was so sharp that it pierced right through the middle of the tart and stuck out on the other side. Fairy was rather ashamed of them, but she remembered they were only a little Bear and a little Brownie. At last she allowed them to reappear on a solemn promise of good behaviour.

"Mother, how often may these nice Boys come and play?" asked the Rich Little Girl in ecstasy. "Every Saturday," said Mother, who was enjoying the fun too. "On Saturdays I shall make it a point to absent myself!" said Great-Aunt Priscilla, with dignity. "Hurrah!" cried Bruno rudely. He really had no manners. How they all loved the magic lantern, and the Xmas Tree. Next there was dancing, and Jasper played for them on his flute. Wouldn't you love to

The Little Green Road to Fairyland

dance with a Bear, a Bunny, a Kookaburra, or a Brownie, if you are a little girl, on a floor slippery as glass; or, if you are a boy, with so sweet a partner as Fairy or Sylvie? But the jolliest thing of all was the grand Brownie Flying Match. Gumkin had thought of a new and cheap kind of aeroplane, namely, soap-bubbles, which if large and strong enough, would be as convenient for mortals as for Brownies. The Brownies gave a wonderful flying display, sitting tight on the bubbles as they revolved, till the spectators grew giddy to see them whirling round and round, and often sitting upside down on the shining iridescent bubbles. Even in that position Winky would close his eye at Great-Aunt Priscilla. In every race Gumkin won, and there was not a single accident.

"Now," said Gumkin, airily alighting from his bubble, "if I produce an extra large bubble, who will volunteer a flight?"

Bruno was the first to volunteer, for he was beginning to be a little jealous of the Brownies. So Gumkin produced a very large bubble, and Bruno sat proudly on top, and sailed round and round the room. But he was a heavy little fellow; suddenly there was a loud bang. Bruno, oh, where was he? The glengarry landed on Great-Aunt Priscilla's head, and Bruno was shot through the ballroom window right into the duck-pond!

This was fortunate; for had he landed on terra firma after such a violent explosion, he must have exploded too. The Rich Little Girl fussed over him

64

so lovingly that, when the shock was over a little, Bruno was quite glad the accident had happened. They all went home to burrow, nest and bed after a lovely time, and said they would be back for more fun early next Saturday.

Chapter 18

The Battle of the Imps and Brownies

> "Marching along, fifty score strong,
> Great-hearted gentlemen, singing this song."
>
> R. BROWNING.

FAIRY kept her Mother's cottage so neat and clean that it was a joy to look at it. Every morning in summer she placed a vase of fresh red roses on the little table by Mary's chair, for Mary was growing very frail now; and on frosty days she saw that the logs burned brightly, and filled the kettle and set it on the blaze, where it shone like gold, for it was of burnished copper.

One evening as they sat in this peaceful happiness, with Kexy on the floor at their feet, and Dicky on a perch overhead, with his head under his wing, a knock came at the door. "Run quickly," said Mary. "It may be some neighbour in distress."

Fairy opened the door, and Gumkin ran in, panting and exhausted. Fairy fanned him, as he told bit by bit his exciting story. "The Cannibal Imps," he said, "came to Tranquillity Farm and stole the Baby, little

The Little Green Road to Fairyland

Kay, from his cradle. Koa, their chief, has put him in a mushroom-ring to plump him up for eating at the Great Feast of Full Moon to-morrow night." Mary and Fairy turned pale, for little Kay was Robin's and Maykin's baby brother. No wonder the Cannibal Imps wanted to eat so sweet a morsel! "We are marching on them in full array!" said Gumkin. "Will you come? As you are a Fairy, and we may resort to camouflage, you will be very useful." Mary and Fairy gladly agreed; for little Kay was in deadly peril. So Fairy set out with Gumkin. The Brownies in marching order were marshalled in the gully; Winky was the drummer-boy. Their weapons were bows and poisoned arrows. All night they marched up the gully, and all the next day, scarcely halting more than a few seconds to eat some wild raspberries or drink the clear crystal water of the creek. It was a race against time, for that was the very night of Full Moon. Fairy was armed with her magic wand. At last, as evening drew on, they could hear, faint and far off, the cannibal tom-toms drumming. "We shall have to approach within close quarters," said Gumkin. "Otherwise we cannot locate the mushroom-ring."

"We can do that easily enough," said Fairy, "for if we all become invisible, we can enter their camp unobserved, steal little Kay, and shoot them with our poisoned arrows. Thus we can conquer them by strategy rather than open fight."

"The reserve forces, meanwhile," said Gumkin, "will remain in the rear to shoot the Moon supposing

The Battle of the Imps and Brownies

she becomes full, and our other plan fails. If she pops out like a pricked bubble, the feast must be put off till next Full Moon." This also seemed a wise manœuvre.

The main army, therefore, became invisible, and entered the camp, where Fairy and Winky went ahead to reconnoitre for Kay and the mushroom-ring. The others stood at a distance out of range.

Now Fairy and Winky were so near they could see the Cannibal Imps holding a corroboree round blazing fires. They had ruby-red eyes like red-hot sparks, and their black bodies were pipeclayed all over with circles, dots and zigzags of pink, white, and yellow. They were hurling showers of boomerangs and nullahs, and wampishing their spears. Fairy and Winky hid behind a gum-sapling to watch. But then Fairy thought, " Poor little Kay !" and they continued to search for him. Just then the great round yellow Moon came out full in the sky, and by its light they saw little Kay sitting on the moss in a mushroom-ring and calmly sucking his thumb. " Little Kay ! Little Kay !" crooned Fairy. " Keep still. Do not fear. Fairy is coming !" But her heart was beating very fast, because of the Full Moon. When the Imps saw the Moon, with a wild howl they all rushed towards the Baby. It was impossible for Fairy to make them all disappear quickly enough ; the only way was to make Kay invisible. She touched his heart with the wand, and, when the Cannibals reached the mushroom-ring, no Baby was there, though they could hear one crying. Fairy hushed his sobs, and at that moment Gumkin shot an arrow clean through the Moon. She disappeared like a pricked bubble. Then, while the Cannibal Imps were dumb with amazement, the Brownies showered poisoned arrows on them, till not one Cannibal Imp was left to tell the tale in all that gully.

They made a little bark canoe to float Kay down the creek, as he was rather heavy for Fairy to carry. Kay slept peacefully all night; the Brownies towed the canoe along from the bank, and Fairy walked beside it singing lullabies. It was an eerie journey all down the gully in the darkness, with the Moon put out. They could hear the Bunyip bellowing from his lair deep in the forest, and the Willy-willies rushing through the tree-tops to carry away lost children. But at dawn the sun pushed his golden fingers through the green gloom. Faint and far off they heard Robin and Maykin calling "Cooee"; "Cooee" they answered, till the gully rang. So at last they reached the dear little mia-mia, and Robin and Maykin took Kay home to Tranquillity Farm.

You may be sure they were all ready for breakfast, and Gumkin was the Hero of the Hour. No one was wounded, except that Winky had to have his cheeky eye bandaged; a boomerang hit it during the corroboree. The Brownies brought home plenty of war trophies—shields, nullahs, boomerangs, necklaces of red berries. Later, as Fairy played in the gully with Robin and Maykin, she said: "Next New Moon I will take you to the Fairy Ball."

THEY SAW LITTLE KAY SITTING ON THE MOSS IN A
MUSHROOM-RING

Chapter 19

Dance of the Fairies

"On the tawny sands and shelves
  Trip the pert fairies and the dapper elves;
  By dimpled brook and fountain brim
  The wood-nymphs, decked with daisies trim,
  Their merry wakes and pastimes keep:
  What hath night to do with sleep?"

Comus.

IT was Full Moon.   Lady Moon sailed silvery and bright, as if to say no Brownie could put her out for long.   "Sh!" said Maykin, as she and Robin crept stealthily out of bed in their little nightgowns. "All is lost, if anyone wakens!"   But as they tiptoed past Mother's door, a little figure met them in the passage.   It had shining eyes, tossed yellow hair, and such a smile, as if to say "Please take me too! You *couldn't* leave me all alone at home!"   "Trust a Baby to know when any Fairy thing is about!" said Maykin. "Robin, we can carry him pick-a-back in turns; but, Kay, you must stay near us and not get lost, or the big Bunyip will catch you."

So Robin took Kay on his back, for it was clear he could not be left behind.   He would have roused the whole house in a few seconds.

In the gully Fairy was waiting near the mia-mia, which looked beautiful as the Moon peeped at it through the tree-ferns, and kissed the Rose Bush and the Cherry-Tree, the Bubble-Tree and the Tree of

69

The Little Green Road to Fairyland

Song-Birds. All the Song-Birds were asleep with heads tucked under wing, but at the Moon's kiss they fluttered their feathers and burst into a carol of joy. The pathway of the little mia-mia was of silver pebbles bordered with scarlet shells, and to-night they were all singing from their deep hearts the remembrance-song of the great sea. The bushes of wild bluebells were singing Fairy chimes, and all the gully was wide awake with rapture for the dance of the Fairies. "Gumkin and the Bush Boys have gone long ago!" said Fairy. "We must hurry ; for, you know, mortals must leave the dance at twelve of the clock. The Fairies stay till cock-crow."

"We are a little late," Robin said, "for Kay is rather heavy."

Fairy led them along the green gully ; they hopped from mossy stone to mossy stone under the tree-ferns and musk and wild lilac, and the creek sang merrily as they went. By-and-by they turned into a little grass track glistening with dew and starred with daisies, under the gum-trees. "We had better leave Kay," said Fairy, "till we find a good place to hide. He is such a chatterbox ! We must not appear at this ball, you know. The Fairies always have their sweetest dances when no mortal is by, and they must not know we are near."

"Oh, Fairy !" cried Maykin. "If we leave Kay he will cry, and the Bunyip will get him."

"He will be safe and happy," Fairy said ; "we will leave him on soft grass in a ring of bunnies."

70

Dance of the Fairies

So Kay was left, in a ring of dear bunnies, laughing and crooning.

The path opened into a mossy glade, near where Fairy's wild violets grew. The moonshiny night was full of their fragrance. "We are in time!" Fairy whispered. "The dance is not begun. This is a good hidy-hole." It was a wee hollow full of ferns, big enough for Bunnies to snuggle in, or very little children cuddled close together. Robin ran back and fetched Kay. It was just as well; for the minute the bunnies heard his footstep rustle in the bracken, they scampered off down their burrows. What if it had been the Bunyip? Robin hugged Kay. They just fitted into the little ferny place, and looked like four birds in a nest.

"I am worried about Kay!" Maykin said. "He is sure to call out when the Fairies come."

"Hadn't you better make his voice go?" asked Robin. "Just for a little! Kay will not mind, will you, Kay?" Kay nodded his head for "No!"

So Fairy touched his little pink tongue with her wand, and Kay's voice vanished. They were just in time. Sweet twitterings and flutterings of flutes sounded afar, coming nearer and nearer, silvery and delicate, like dream-music in the Moon. Then the Fairies came; their loveliness took the children's breath away. For they danced with the grace of tossing flowers in the wind, or the light leaping of foam on the white-crested waves. Wherever their feet touched the sod, buds opened, toadstools peeped,

71

little blue eggs appeared, and out of them broke fairy birds, no bigger than bees, with jewelled wings. Nearer and nearer to the hollow the Fairies danced, circling round and round. Then, unclasping hands a minute, they folded the children in a ring of Fairies, and the dance went on.

This shows, of course, that mortals cannot hide from Fairies, though Fairies almost always hide from mortals. That is fair, because all Fairies believe in mortals, but almost no mortals believe in Fairies, and so they cannot see them.

As the Fairies spun round they sang a little song, and the song wove a wreath of dream-flowers round the children—the very flowers the Fairies had garlanded round Robin and Maykin at the beginning of the story. It meant, you remember, that they belonged for ever to the Fairies and had Fairy eyes. And now Kay was in the magic ring too. As the Fairies danced, they began to chant this little croon :

" Fairy child in the ferns,
  Mortal heart glows and burns—
  Heart that gave flute and wings
  All for love, Fairy things !
  Yield us now wand as well
  Ere we cast Fairy spell ;
  Fairy wand if you keep,
  Evermore shall you sleep ;
  Fairy wand if you give,
  Evermore shall you live.
  Lo ! our Queen bade us say
  Fairy Child cannot stay ;
  Fairy Child soon must roam,
  Seeking far Fairy home ;

THEN THE FAIRIES CAME

Dance of the Fairies

Heart and key, lost and gone,
Seeking far, on and on;
Following on, far and far,
Fairyland's shimmering star."

As they sang, Fairy knew it was her call home from the Queen of the Fairies, and that soon she must go. Somehow, somewhere, she would find her heart and the golden key and cross the space to Fairyland. But there was a long, long way to go, and she must go all alone; only her mortal heart was left her now, and even the wand was to be taken.

"Dear Fairies," she cried, "before I give it, let me make Kay speak again." "No, I will give him a Fairy gift!" said the loveliest of all the Fairies. And taking the wand, she touched Kay's lips with her own, and said: "He shall be a great poet and sing wonders never heard before! For now he can talk, but now it is the Fairy speech!"

Then they all smiled very sadly at Fairy and said: "Little sister, we shall meet again soon in Fairyland, but first you must find your Fairy heart and the little gold key of the little green door."

"The little green door?" thought Fairy. But she was wise enough not to ask questions. She knew that all in good time she would understand.

Now the Fairies vanished; only the wistful moonlight and the fragrance of violets flooded the glade. Kay's drowsy eyes closed, and he slumbered peacefully as they carried him safe home to his cradle.

Then Fairy walked home pensively, and in the

L
73

cottage Mary was asleep, very pale and still; Fairy kissed her softly, and Mary's lips opened, and she said " Lily." " She will soon go," said Fairy, gazing at her sorrowfully, " to the Big Man and Lily. Then I shall be all alone, and it will be time to set out on my long journey. How can I find Fairyland? I am more a child now than ever, for my flute and wings and wand are gone. Where shall I find the Fairy heart and the little gold key?"

Chapter 20

Mary Goes Away

" Shy one, shy one,
Shy one of my heart,
She moves in the firelight
Pensively apart."
W. B. YEATS.

AFTER this Fairy never left Mary's side; day and night she stayed near her, doing a thousand little acts of thoughtfulness and love, and Mary's beautiful eyes would smile at her with a mother-look that made Fairy feel happy and yet lonely. These were the sweet days of summertime; the sunlight lay like a golden hush over the forest and the gully. A thousand red roses blossomed on the two bushes on either side of the door, and a thousand lilies filled the little garden with perfume. Dicky and Kexy stayed near the cottage, too, these days; and Gumkin

and the Bush Boys were constant visitors. Fairy loved
them to come, for always they could make Mary
laugh. Besides, they were very useful; they swept
and dusted and washed and ironed, and Fairy baked
them lovely little scones and cakes in payment. She
was more like an ordinary little girl now, as she had
no flute, no wings, and no wand. She could not do
such wonderful Fairy things; and yet her mortal heart,
along with her Fairy eyes, helped her to be more of
a Fairy, in some ways, than before. For, one day, a
little mother bunny was shot dead with a bang-fire
stick as she was hurrying home with a lettuce for her
three babies' supper; Robin carried her in to Fairy, with
Maykin crying beside him. Fairy whispered into the
bunny's ear, and stroked her fur. Very soon she sat
up, and began to wiggle her whiskers and rub her nose
with her paws. "Thank you, dear children," she
said. "Someday, it may be, I shall help you. But
now I must run; the babies will be crying for supper."
So off she scampered through the door. Another day
Sylvie came running in pale and trembling, her old
ragged frock gathered up in her arms. "What is it?"
said Mary anxiously. And Fairy put her arms about
her, as she burst into tears. Poor little Sylvie had
climbed over into the field of Miser Flintskin and
filled her frock with his potatoes. She did not think
there was any harm; he had so many, and it did not
occur to Sylvie she was doing wrong. The crimson
heath, the yellow wattle, the white daisies were lovelier
far than potatoes, and God was not angry when she

75

gathered great armfuls of His flowers. Only men, it seemed, grudged a share of the good things they possessed. And Sylvie's daddy was so very ill, and there was no food in the cabin.

"Hush!" said Fairy, hugging Sylvie closer. "Do not say a word. Just stay with me." Now they could hear Miser Flintskin shuffling up the path and muttering: "'Possums! 'Possums! Queer kind of 'Possums! I've got her now, and out of the cabin they go, sick or well, and lucky not to be in gaol!" He knocked on the door with his stick, and pushed past Fairy into the cottage. Then roughly he ordered Sylvie to unfold her frock and show what she was hiding. But Sylvie's torn frock held only a drift of wild flowers, and the old miser shuffled off a little ashamed of himself. But when Robin and Maykin told their mother about this, she went to the cabin, and took Sylvie and her father home to live at Tranquillity Farm, where there was warmth and food and joy and comfort.

Meanwhile Gumkin had been improving his bubble airships and making them bigger and stronger. He made a special one for Sylvie, which not only floated in the air, but revolved with glorious pictures in all colours of the rainbow. It was a lovely sight to watch Sylvie in her Fairy frock floating on the great bubble. Sometimes she floated right over the tree-tops across the gully to visit Mary and Fairy, and Mary had a happy time, though she was weak and ill. Gumkin and Winky lived at the cottage now to do the housework

SYLVIE IN HER FAIRY FROCK FLOATING
ON THE GREAT BUBBLE.

and run messages, while Fairy nursed her mother and cooked the meals. Bruno, not to be outdone by his rival, acted as sentry up in the tallest gum-tree near the cottage. He had a good deal to put up with at first. A mother magpie pecked his nose with her hard, sharp beak, thinking he had come to rob her nest; then Gran'dad Kookaburra laughed at his glengarry, if he ever wore it; the yellow-crested Cockatoo bit his paw when he peeped into the hollow window of the gum-tree to say "Hello!" and the wild bees stung him all over. But soon the other residents of the gum-tree became acquainted with him, and no one could help loving Bruno. He had such quaint and comical ways. He found another hollow in the tree-trunk, and made a bed in it of moss and leaves and fluff; there were plenty of tender young gum-shoots to nibble. So Bruno was useful, busy, and happy. Jasper came to the cottage, too, just once to say good-bye. He played a farewell song on the magic flute, for he was going with it to the Golden City in the Big World to win fame and fortune. "But I will never forget you, Fairy!" he said, and he never did. John came once, and his face was very grave as he kissed Fairy good-bye. Then came the Princess with her Prince, but when they came the cottage was empty; Mary was with Lily, and Fairy was gone.

For one sunny dawn Mary could not hear her little girl, though Fairy whispered "Mother!" in her ear, and kissed her eyes, and hugged her tight round the neck. Then the bells rang again—the praying bells—

and Mary went away. Fairy knew she had gone to
the Big Man and Lily. So Fairy said good-bye to the
dear little earth home she had loved so long, and,
closing the door, she took Dicky and Kexy, and
wandered down to the bank of wild violets, where she
had first alighted from Fairyland.

"I have done all a Fairy can," she told them, " to
help the Big World. Some of the Mortals would not
even see me, and others could not. Mother has gone
home to her Big Man and Lily; her lovely eyes are
gone. The Prince has ridden away with the Princess.
Robin and Maykin are in the Fairy Ring, and little
Kay has the Fairy Kiss. Sylvie has my wings and
Jasper the flute, and there will be no more cane or
dunce's cap in the little school for ever any more. But
my mortal heart is paining me, and, oh, I want to
find my Fairy heart, and the little gold key to unlock
the little green door to Fairyland." Each of the
violets had a tear in its eye; but their fragrance had
never before been so sweet, for perfume is the love of
flowers. Then Fairy begged the violets to care for
Kexy and Dicky, as she must set out on her long way
to Fairyland. This the violets gladly promised to do.
So, when Fairy had kissed them all good-bye, until
they should meet again in Fairyland, she set out to find
the little gold key to open the little green door to
Fairyland. "Good-bye, little namesakes!" she called,
as she kissed her hand to them and waved till she was
out of sight.

Then she sat down under a great gum-tree and

78

cried. For she was all alone in the wide world. What was a poor little Fairy to do, lost so far from Fairyland? "This will never do!" she told herself at last, jumping up briskly. "There must be *some* way, for the Fairy Queen sent me a message at the Dance of the Fairies to seek, very hard, my little gold key and my Fairy home."

Chapter 21

The Long Green Tunnel

"The wind blows out of the gates of the day,
The wind blows over the lonely of heart,
And the lonely of heart is withered away,
Where the faeries dance in a place apart."
W. B. YEATS.

FAIRY went to the little mia-mia in the gully first, but it was a very tumbled-down place now. Only the beautiful tree-fern that made the roof was undamaged. For Fairy had been long away, and the others had had no heart to play there without her. At the four corners there was no Rose-bush and Cherry-bush, no Bubble-tree or Tree of Song-birds, and the bluebells were shrivelled and withered. Only the gully stretched upward away out of sight, a tunnel of cool green gloom, and the creek murmured on and on.

"It *must* be up the gully!" thought Fairy. "It is time to begin my adventures!" The moment she

79

entered the gully, she saw a most beautiful yellow flower, poised on a tall slender stem, beside the creek. She stooped to look at it closer, for the gully was dark; and she saw it was a butterfly with filmy golden wings, dazzling as sunshine; the butterfly flew on up the gully, and Fairy followed eagerly, hopping lightly from stone to stone, though often she nearly slipped on the damp moss. Sometimes the butterfly would pause to let her catch up; then it fluttered on faster than ever. The creek seemed to be singing, "Follow, Fairy! Follow, Fairy!" After a while the blue sky and sunshine peeped through the over-arching trees, and the gully opened into a ferny dell, where the butterfly danced about with the sunbeams till Fairy could not distinguish it from one. She reached the dell and there she found Robin and Maykin waiting for her, and playing merry games with Bruno, Gumkin, and Winky. The Baby Bunnies were there too, and the little Kookaburras all in a row on a branch. Fairy's heart gave a great leap of joy to see her little friends again.

"We came here to wait for you!" said Robin. "From the tree-tops Bruno saw you enter the gully, and we floated here on bubbles to take you home."

"Do, do come home and be our little sister!" Maykin begged, putting her arms round Fairy. They had a little picnic spread out for Fairy on the grass among the daisies. There were sandwiches and jam-tarts, a plum-cake, strawberries and cream, and sugarsticks, and a billy boiling for tea on a bright fire. They had

The Long Green Tunnel

a merry day, climbed, romped, sang, and played all the
dear old games. Hide-and-seek was great fun, popping
in and out of the burrows with the Bunnies, and
peeping from the leafy branches up with the Kookaburras. But at last Bruno, who had climbed to the
tip-top of a bluegum, called out, "Someone is moving
up the gully with a candle!" "Oh, it is my butterfly!"
cried Fairy, in distress. "I must go at once!" "No!
no!" said the others. "Stay and be just a little girl
with us!" "I cannot!" Fairy answered. "The
butterfly is a messenger from the Fairy Queen to guide
me to Fairyland, and I must follow." "Take us with
you, then!" begged Robin and Maykin. "I will take
you a little way, but you cannot go far." "Why not
be sensible everyday folks like us?" said Bruno.
"The world all round us is full of fun and frolic.
"Stay and rest and enjoy life. We are the Children
of To-day."

"No," Fairy answered, "the call has come from
Fairyland, and I must go." "Then in that case," said
Bruno, "while *you* explore, which strikes me as foolish,
I will stay and finish the picnic, and we can clear up
and carry home the baskets." But though his voice
was careless, he sniffed and rubbed his furry arm across
his eyes a good many times as he saw Fairy vanish with
Robin and Maykin. The butterfly now seemed to be
a sunbeam gliding slowly up the green tunnel. It
shone with unearthly lustre and radiance, so that at
times it dazzled their eyes. At last it lighted on the
moss, sparkling with dewdrops, and filled the space

around with soft light. "It is a glow-worm," said Robin. "I have often read about them. I should love to see it close and hold it in my hand."

They stooped to pick up the glow-worm; Robin could not catch it; Maykin could not catch it. It slipped like sunlight through their fingers. But when Fairy put her little hand under it, the radiance seemed only a halo shining above a fair round pearl of wonderful beauty which lay in her palm. It was soft as a dove's breast and lustrous as moonlight. And, dimly, under the surface strange mystic pictures seemed to move and a light pulsed deep within. "The Fairy heart!" whispered Robin and Maykin. Just then the pearl vanished, and in Fairy's palm lay a lovely red rose-bud. They knew the Fairy heart had returned to her and she had lost her mortal heart. "You must leave me now, darling, darling little Brother and Sister," Fairy said to the children. "Now I cannot stay, for I am a Fairy again, lost in the Big World. I must find the little green door and its golden key before cockcrow, or I shall never reach Fairyland."

Maykin began to cry, and Robin looked near it.

"Hush!" said Fairy. "I will give you my mortal heart. Treasure it always. It will be a bond of love between us and never fade. Look how already the petals begin to unfold."

So then they talked a little longer, and kissed good-bye, and Robin and Maykin, with the mortal heart, turned homeward down the gully; but Fairy, with her magic heart, climbed higher and higher up the gully, where the little pale golden halo led her on.

Chapter 22

Adventures by the Way

> " Ere it vanishes
> Over the margin,
> After it, follow it,
> Follow the gleam !"
> TENNYSON.

FAIRY often missed her little friends as she walked steadily on. It nearly made her cry to think of Mary and the little cottage, of Tranquillity Farm, of Winky's eye and Bruno's patch. Luckily she had to keep her eye so steadily on the golden disk of light, dancing ahead of her, that there was no time to be sad. As the gully grew denser, the shining disk grew brighter. Fairy then saw that it was a radiant star beckoning her on. Fairy was glad to go ; she felt happy now, and her magic heart danced for joy.` She had done all she could to help the Big World, and there was nothing to keep her there any more. She began to feel wild and light again, like one of the forest elves at the moonlight dance. The star shone over a little round pool of water, and made it so lovely that Fairy danced round the little pool in rapture until she was weary ; then stooped down and gazed in it, to see looking up at her a little eager face,

and the star far away down in the water. "Must I
follow there?" asked Fairy. And the little girl
looked up at her wistfully and begged "Come!"
Fairy stretched out her arms to clasp her and their lips
met in a kiss, when the water suddenly became grey,
and little ripples shivered over it; no star was there,
and the sweet-faced child of the pool was gone.
"Where are you, O beautiful star?" called Fairy.
"Cooee! Where are you?" "Cooee! where are
you?" answered a clear voice, and a lovely child, with
eyes grey as Dawn, stepped from the slender white-
stemmed gum-saplings that crowned the gully. She
was dressed like the little Greek girls Fairy had seen
in books; her robe was the misty-blue of hills far
away, silver sandals were on her feet, and round her
head a wreath of smoke-blue gum-leaves. Fairy had
never seen a child so pale: like the snow on the
winter hills she was; only her lips were red as holly-
berries, and her voice called through them like a silver
bell. "Did you see him?" she asked Fairy. "I
have waited so long, and I thought you must see him
in the pool."

"Who are you, little Stranger?" said Fairy gently.

"I am Echo," she said. "Long ago my little
sweetheart, Narcissus, looked into that pool, and what
he saw there I cannot tell; but he gazed and gazed,
and could not be coaxed away; in the end he was
changed to a daffodil, leaning over the water to peep
at its mirrored beauty; long ago the daffodil faded,
but some day Narcissus will come back to me, and we

shall wander over the hills together home." "Will you come with me to find Fairyland?" asked Fairy. "It cannot be far, but my star, too, is lost, and we will seek Fairyland together. For your Narcissus is surely there." "No, I will wait!" Echo said gravely. "He will not go without me. But see, your star is yonder." The star came out above the little gum-trees, and began to move onwards and upwards. "Goodbye," called Fairy, running. And as she followed the star she called "Cooee!" and Echo answered, till they heard each other no more.

Presently the creek widened into a little lake, too deep for Fairy to wade across, but the star moved right over it and halted in the middle. "Dear me!" thought Fairy in dismay. "I hope it is not Will o' the Wisp after all. What shall I do?"

It was too far to run round the margin of the lake, and, in any case, there were very steep cliffs on each side, and no path was visible. But a great host of frogs leapt out of the water and croaked at her. She would have liked to turn and run—they looked so fierce, but she was afraid she would lose sight of her starry guide. So she said politely, "Could you direct me across the lake, gentle Frog?"

"With pleasure, Princess!" said the leader of the frogs, bowing low and laying his hand on his heart. "We regret startling you. But we are the Scouts of His Majesty, King Croak the Millionth. We feared an enemy was approaching. Will you sit upon this lily-leaf, with the water-lily for a cushion, and we will tow you safely over?" Fairy gladly obeyed; for she trusted the little frogs. So she sailed smoothly along to the middle of the lake, when an unlucky accident happened. A Kookaburra seeing so many frogs within grasp swooped down, and they all had to dive for their lives. Fairy was much alarmed; but, as she struggled in the water, reassuring bubbles came up from beneath humbly apologising and promising safe convoy for the rest of the voyage. "It is well for frogs," said the leader, as they helped her once more to embark on the lily-leaf, "that we are a kind of natural submarine. We constantly have to dive to avoid these combined torpedo-destroyers and aeroplanes. I refer, you understand, to what you call Ducks, and Kookaburras, and other such queer craft. Croak! croak! croak! We therefore constantly resort to camouflage, such as these green mottled suits! Croak! croak! croak!"

"Plonk! Plonk! Plonk!" sounded a deep voice from the pool. "Whoever is that?" said Fairy, turning pale. "Have no fear!" said the courteous Frog. "Our King wishes to know if you will rest a while in his Palace ere you continue your pilgrimage. He is renowned for hospitality to strangers and pilgrims to far lands."

"Fain would I tarry," said Fairy, "but my star calls me on!" "Aha! the pilot-light!" said the Frog. "Farewell, then, lovely Stranger, and a speedy home-coming!" By this time Fairy was feeling more and more of a Fairy, and less and less of a little girl. So

her drenched clothes very quickly dried in a truly
Fairy fashion, and she hastened her steps to keep up
with the star.

Chapter 23

The Children of Golden Dreams

"The dream that fires man's heart to make,
To build, to do, to sing or say,
A beauty Death can never take."

JOHN MASEFIELD.

SOMETIMES the star rested awhile high up in the
tree-tops or floated on a cloud.   Then Fairy rested
too.   Often she found wild raspberries growing, or
strawberry bushes thick with scarlet fruit, or strange
lovely flowers brimming with milk and honey.   Sometimes she found Fairy bread, which Mortals call
manna.

They reached a sunny place where the water
prattled over golden pebbles, and the banks were
yellow with mists of wattle-blossom like sunlight.
From the bank of golden sand two lovely fair children
were launching little boats, which sailed away bravely
down the stream.   The children had pale gold hair;
and they seemed to be all made of light, so luminous,
frail, and unsubstantial was their form.   Round their
throats hung necklaces of golden shells, chiming and
murmuring of their unforgotten sea.   Sometimes Fairy
thought she was mistaken, that no children were there,

87

but only slim wisps of sunshine. They looked at her earnestly a moment, and then gravely continued their play, too joyously absorbed to smile.

"If you please, what are you doing?" asked Fairy softly, stepping up to the children; they were a little boy and a little girl. "Sailing our little boats," said the boy, without looking up. "I know, but what is in them?" "Some have dreams," he said, "and others questions. See, this little boat is full of dreams!" and Fairy saw that the little boat was full of golden buds. "And this," he said, "is full of questions." And the boat was laden with small golden seeds. "Where are they going?" asked Fairy. "Down to the Great Sea," he said; "and some day we too shall follow." "Who are you?" she said. "For surely you must be the Son and Daughter of the King." "We are the children of Golden Dreams," he answered. "I am Vision and she is Fancy. In the distance, far away across the Great Sea, lies the Golden City, where dreams come true; there our little boats are bound, there the seeds will waken and the buds unfold. We are the Children of To-morrow." But Fairy thought, "How many of the little boats will be wrecked! How many of those golden flowers will fade, and the seeds perish, long, long before they reach the Great Sea!" So in pity for the children and the wreckage of their Golden Dreams, she said, "Come with me! Follow the star to Fairyland!" "No," he said, and Fancy smiled gravely, and shook her head. "We go the other way into the Golden Future. For we are the Children of To-morrow."

"The Dreams will not *all* be wrecked," said Fairy to herself; "*some* will reach the Golden City, and the questions will some day be answered." She then bade the beautiful children farewell; but they scarcely noticed, so intent they were on their Fairy flotilla. So Fairy slowly turned away, on and up the gully, following the star.

Chapter 24

Golden Mountain

"He gives nothing but worthless gold."—LOWELL.

NOW the gully was becoming dark, and evening was drawing in. The star kindly sank lower, and moved forward on a level with Fairy's eyes. This was pleasant and comforting in the green gloom. At last, as if weary, the star sank on to the moss, and rested there with a dull glow. Fairy eagerly sprang forward, anxious to handle and see clearly this Fairy guide of such changeful shape. It seemed like a golden topaz, full of light, as it lay on her palm; but suddenly the light dulled and died. A tiny nugget of pure gold lay in her hand. Fairy looked at it with much pleasure. "How glad the charcoal-burner would be," she thought, "to know of this. *I* think the golden buttercups are far lovelier, but I know men prize these yellow stones. This must be the Golden Mountain

of the Gnomes, who live beneath the earth and hide
the rich gold in tiny channels underground. Was it
to this my star was guiding me, to help my dear
friends in the Big World?" Then she wondered if
she should go back to Tranquillity Farm with a
message about the yellow gold; and yet, if she went,
maybe she would lose her star and never win home to
Fairyland at all. What was a poor little lost Fairy to
do? "Anyway, this little yellow stone will not help
me!" she thought. "I would gladly give it in return
for a little crusty yellow loaf, like the ones Mother
baked at home." At that she burst into tears; for
what was a little wandering forlorn Fairy to do?
Suddenly she heard shrill voices chanting in chorus:

> "Gold, gold, rare, rich gold,
> More than the King's tall towers can hold;
> Gold, gold, fair, fine gold,
> Deep in the mountain, down in the mould;
> Follow, come, follow us deep down deep,
> Where the grey gnomes delve and the death-worms creep,
> And we need no torches under the mould,
> For the light is bright of the yellow gold!"

A little procession of grey gnomes, with hooked
noses and speckled capes, flitted by; they carried
sacks of small gold nuggets, and their eyes were
smouldering tawny yellow, like the eyes of owls by
night. They jerked out their marching-song in
cracked voices more like the hooting of owls than
anything else Fairy had heard. When they saw Fairy,
they suddenly wheeled round, stood at attention in a

row, and, bowing, laid the sacks of gold at her feet. Then silently, in a line, they trooped into a hollow moss-covered log and disappeared. " I will follow and explore !" Fairy thought, " for my star is gone ;" and, at the words, as she peeped into the hollow log, a torch flared red at the far end, like an angry spark, and then vanished. Fairy crept along the log on hands and knees. " I must make haste or I shall miss my light," she said to herself. At the far end of the log was a little tunnel overgrown with tiny yellow toadstools and ferns and moss; the tunnel began to descend, and its sides were very slippy. Bats hovered about with shrill squeaks, and Fairy was very much afraid she would tread on a snake. But at last she reached the bottom of the slanting tunnel and walked along a small opening, at the end of which was a cave. In the dimness Fairy could distinguish the dull glimmer of gold, and of phantom shapes circling round with pattering feet and chanting in a whisper the song she heard above ground. " What does it all mean ?" she wondered. Then, as her eyes grew accustomed to the dark, she noticed that the gnomes were vanishing one by one through a dark opening in the side of the cave. Fairy followed and stood in the opening. Within was a great cavern lit by flaring torches ; on a blazing furnace bubbled flat pans of molten gold, which the gnomes were pouring busily from tiny kettles of burnished copper into narrow veins in the rocky cavern walls. The gold flowed away deep into the secret heart of the mountain, hidden far

The Little Green Road to Fairyland

from the grasping hands of Mortals. Spellbound, Fairy watched the trickling gold, as it hissed into its slender channels like golden snakes. At last one of the gnomes, who seemed to be the overseer, turned his yellow blinking eyes upon her, and said in his cracked voice : "Well?" "Well!" said Fairy, not knowing what else to say. "Do you like this?" he asked. "It is very pretty, sir!" Fairy answered, wishing to please the little man. "Pretty! pretty! What is *that*?" he said, excitedly snapping his fingers. "I mean, would you like to own all this?" "I think not!" Fairy replied gravely. "Thank you very much all the same. But if you please, I would rather have a little crusty loaf and a cup of milk!" "Seize her!" shrieked the gnome to his brothers. "Bind her with golden chains! Keep her in our cavern for our Queen! She is a Fairy. She can turn all we bring to gold. She can turn to rich, rare gold the yellow wattle and the bright buttercups, dancing sunbeams and maidens' shining tresses, the sunset and the evening star—aye, and the gleaming hopes and burning hearts of Mortals. Bind her; chain her! Remember the fine, fair gold; we shall have the wide world to smelt in our furnace." A thousand yellow eyes glared at Fairy, a thousand shadow-shapes leapt upon her, she heard quick breathing all about her; then a wonderful thing happened. Suddenly a radiant light filled all the horrible cavern, so dazzling that the gnomes crouched back against the walls with their arms across their eyes, blinded; and even Fairy could

"KEEP HER IN OUR CAVERN FOR OUR QUEEN!"

not see for a moment. But she knew it was her star, and that in her weariness and hunger she had mistaken the false light for the true. The radiant light swiftly withdrew from the cavern, seeming to beckon Fairy after it. They reached the little cave, then the sloping tunnel; the star shot up it like a meteor, and Fairy stumbled after as swiftly as she could, and so along the hollow log into the gully. Then she dared to look back, and from the log came the wicked gleam of yellow eyes, the wafture of angry hands, and the chattering of cracked voices in argument. Fairy ran along the gully after the star as fast as her legs could carry her. It was now deep twilight, almost night; but the bright star paused above a little warm nest in the brown bracken. There, spread on the moss, Fairy saw a little yellow crusty loaf like Mother's, a mug of milk, and a daisy-chain like the ones she wore in the dear school-meadow at home. Happily Fairy ate and drank; then she said her evening prayers and lay down to sleep. And the star, she was sure, kissed her and blessed her; it seemed to say, "We shall find the little green door to Fairy-land long before cock-crow. Sleep and rest, ere we journey on."

Chapter 25

The Children of Alcheringa, the Long Ago (the Far Past)

" Our hearts stood still in the hush
Of an age gone by."
WALTER DE LA MARE.

LITTLE ALCHERINGA, with her lovely face and graceful form and yearning eyes, sat by the stream just where it gathered its gleaming waters to leap, like a bent glittering bow, down the mountain-steep amid the ferns and clematis and giant eucalypts. She had heard of daring men coming from far off in boats to search for the great Land of the Southern Cross where her tribe had lived so long. Some of these men had lubras and piccaninnies, who were white as the snow on the mountain-tops, with eyes like the blue sky, and hair like the golden sunlight. Little Alcheringa had asked and asked again why none of them had come to play with her; for she would love dearly a little fair playmate. She would show her the hidy-holes of the bunnies; the dance of Buln-Buln, the Lyre-bird; the hollow in the gum-tree where the wild-bee stored her honey; the sea-blue Kingfisher's nest; yes, and the corners where the rarest, loveliest orchids hid. So she waited for the White Child to come with her love and friendship, and questioned the " Wise

94

The Children of Alcheringa

Men" and old chiefs of the tribe; but they looked at one another and smiled. They said, "The Child is beautiful—but she belongs to Alcheri, the Land of Dreams."

But that was long, long ago in the far past; the White Man came and the White Child, but they brought no love for the dark-faced people. Little Alcheringa's tribe dwindled and vanished as she dreamed her dreams by the flowing river. One by one they fell asleep and went to the Shadow-Land; and Alcheringa went to them one day, but still she wandered back, even from the Shadow-Land sometimes, to see the White Child. So it happened—when Fairy awoke from slumber, to find it was dusk and the star was moving onward—she met along the way a little Shadow-Shape with a wreath of pale filmy wattle-blossom, like light, about her hair. The star paused, veiled in a thin mist, and Fairy knew it was safe to stay and talk awhile.

The little Shadow gazed at her with wistful eyes and spoke strange words, which only a Fairy could understand. "Welcome!" they meant. "Little sweet stranger, I have waited long!" So then they played together such happy games. Alcheringa took Fairy up past the waterfall to the round crystal well-spring of the creek, where the water bubbled up from the heart of the everlasting hills. There they saw the two little faces mirrored on the clear surface of the pool, and Alcheringa whispered, "Why are we different?" Then said Fairy, "You belong to Dreamland, I to

The Little Green Road to Fairyland

Fairyland. But let us play together this little while before we part."

"But you are the White Child surely?" said Alcheringa. "You look like my dream come true." "The White Children live below, far down the creek!" answered Fairy. "They are like Angels to look upon, but I am a lost Fairy in search of the little gold key to the little green door of Fairyland. Once I was a mortal-child and dwelt among them; I can tell you of their ways, and do you tell me of yours."

While Fairy was speaking, the hills and the gully and creek were flooded with misty sunlight, such as shines on a morning of frost and dew. Straight away the Bush became peopled with living creatures of wondrous shape and colour. Cockatoos, snow-white, or rose and grey, chattered in the branches; rainbow parrots and azure kingfishers darted hither and thither, while butterflies like living blossoms flitted among the radiant wild-flowers and ferns. Little dainty Blue-bonnet with his tiny brown mate cheeped in the wild lilac-tree, and the Bell-bird carolled sweet and clear. Then Alcheringa led Fairy to a small glade where a little mia-mia stood, made all of bark and branches. She showed Fairy her rug of bunny-skins, and her coverlet of blue, scarlet, and green rosella feathers, her dilly-bag of plaited rushes, and her necklace of shiny red berries. They watched the little fish leaping in the silver rapids and the 'Possum hanging by his tail from a gum-tree bough. Then, as they laughed, another little Shadow-Shape came walking towards them.

The Children of Alcheringa

He was a young, slender boy, and carried a boomerang, nulla, and spear. A little cap of grey fur was on his head, and in it a yellow cockatoo crest. This was Ullu-Kullu, Shooting Star, the Son of the Great Chief of Alcheringa's tribe. All the way from Shadow-Land he followed her, whenever she roamed back to the gully of their childhood. For Ullu-Kullu loved Alcheringa, and had meant, some day, to marry her when he became King of the Tribe. But that was long ago, before the White Man came, and Alcheringa and Ullu-Kullu had both gone too young to the Shadow-Land.

"I will not take her from you," Fairy said gently understanding that he was sorrowful and angry, believing the White Child had come. "Soon I must go to Fairyland; but stay awhile and play. There is time enough before cock-crow." Ullu-Kullu then hurled the boomerang to display his skill; and merrily they laughed to see it wheel back to his feet like a homing pigeon; but Fairy cried when he shot a baby bear. This made the others laugh again. "Why," said he, "it is but a shadow, and the boomerang a shadow. I cannot harm the creatures of the Bush." They then watched Buln-Buln, the lyre-bird, in his graceful dance. But now the mist slowly floated from the star; its bright eye beckoned Fairy on. "Good-bye, little Shadows," she said. "I will come again, between dusk and cock-crow, to play in the gully. Then I shall have Fairy wings again." "Come with us" they eagerly entreated, "to dwell in Shadow-

Land." "It cannot be," answered Fairy, "Shadow-Land is of the Far Past. But we will bridge the space between Shadow-Land and Fairyland with my wings, so that whenever I will I can fly back to you." She watched the two little Shadows flit away among the trees, and then followed the guiding star; and now it was deep night.

Chapter 26

The Little Green Door

"Lands
"Where blaze the unimaginable flowers."
J. E. FLECKER.

"THERE cannot be far to go," Fairy thought. "The Shadow Child showed me the well-spring of the creek, and I must be near the little green door." She was beginning to look a white and weary little Fairy now, but her blue eyes were shining, and her heart felt wonderfully "hopinsidy." She knew something big was to happen soon. The green tunnel had become very narrow; it would have been quite dark, only that the star made light enough for Fairy to see. Now came all kinds of strange frightening movements and flutterings in the thick undergrowth on either side, and soft footsteps padded close behind. But ahead the star moved steadily on. "I will not look behind or sideways," Fairy resolved,

The Little Green Door

though she felt queer things touching and clutching her. Shadows fell across her path, and she felt things peering at her from the dark forest as she moved on; drip-drops of dew fell from the over-arching branches, mopokes hooted, and bats squeaked; Fairy heard all the mysterious whisperings and shufflings of the Little People by night—the Bogles, Hobgoblins, and Kelpies, Warlocks, Sprites, and Ghosties. "I am a Fairy myself!" she remembered. "They cannot harm me unless I yield to them." She actually saw a bat-winged Bogle fly up and catch at her star, as a hawk would snap at a wren. "Ha—ha!" he seemed to cry, "I'll have you yet!" But the radiant star glided calmly on; its brilliance dazzled the Bogle's wicked green eyes.

Then how lovely was the circling dance of the Elves; they swayed like wind-blown white poppies in the moonlight. Fairy was tempted to give up her quest, dance with them hand-in-hand, and forget the little gold key, the little green door, and Fairyland. Sometimes damp and clammy things touched her hands and face. Fairy nearly shrieked, but her brave heart made her quiet. Once Echo's voice, calling "Cooee!" from very far away, startled her; she thought it was cock-crow, and all hope of Fairyland was lost.

At last the star stood still at the very top of the green tunnel. "It must be the little green door!" Fairy thought, and ran up the steep mossy slope. The star now seemed like a candle set in a window. But when Fairy reached the top of the hill, she saw a green mossy wall, and in it a little green mossy door, just big enough for a Fairy or a very young child. In it was a keyhole, and, shining through it, the most wonderful golden light Fairy had ever seen. The star seemed to have slid right through the keyhole! The soft golden light glowed all about Fairy; banks of wild violets grew all round and at her feet. Through the shut door she could hear the twittering of flutes and the fluttering of wings. "This is the little green door!" said she. "But where is the little gold key? I will not peep through the keyhole! No right-principled Fairy would do that, but I wonder where my star has gone?" "Through the keyhole!" a voice seemed to answer. This brought Fairy's eyes back from the violets to the keyhole, and she saw that the light had changed into a tiny burnished key of gold. Quickly she turned it; for it began to quiver with impatience like some living thing, as if to say: "Make haste! Make haste! You will be too late!"

Instantly the little green door opened wide. Fairy stood on a narrow rocky ledge of gold, with a precipice falling sheer away at her feet. She saw stretching away before her a sea of golden light; starry islands were dotted here and there, and floating clouds broke on their shores in soundless waves. There floated the moon-boat along the tide of light with her pearly keel and sails of snow; wide-eyed children were the passengers, and scattered into the Sunset Sea white poppy-buds. "Oh, how shall I cross the sea?" cried Fairy, clasping her hands in distress. "I must think

The Little Green Door

of some way; but first I must shut the little green door. Good-bye, dear green Earth, where I lived and loved and played! Good-bye, little comrades! Some day I will fly back to visit you on my Fairy wings—if ever I have Fairy wings again." She knelt down and gazed through the little green door, along the tunnel, earthwards. Shadows seemed to peer back at her wistfully and stretch out longing arms. But the door closed suddenly with a snap; there was no light in the keyhole. Only a long sigh came through; then a stillness.

"Dear me!" thought Fairy. "I am shut out of Earth and out of Fairyland! I cannot stay perched up here for ever; something must be done. I must try to fly, that's all, without wings. It has probably never been done before, but that is no reason why it should not begin. I rather fancy being a pioneer!"

"Isn't it rather rash to cast oneself into that great abyss in such a lighthearted, reckless style?" asked a curious voice. "I suppose so; but, as I must cast myself, you see, I may as well do it light-heartedly." "In that case," said the funny little man, "you will have an excellent lifebuoy. A light heart is the best kind in a sea of troubles; a heavy heart, you know, would soon sink you! I was just going to offer you my advice, but I see you do not need it." "Indeed, I do," Fairy exclaimed. "But who are you, sir?" "I am Streak o' Lightning!" he answered. "I live on this ledge; it is big enough for the likes o' me; I am so thin and narrow. You've often seen me darting about over the sky and hopping up and down on the edges of clouds." "Please, what do you advise?" interrupted Fairy, who was afraid he had embarked on a long explanation. Fairies hate explanations, because they understand things far more quickly than the explanations of things, for you know, the whole is greater than its part, if you see what this argument means. It *is* a little hazy, though it is really quite clear.

"I was going to offer you the use of my flame-wings," he said. "But I see you do not need them. The Fairy Queen has sent your star to powder your shoulders with star-dust, and the wings are beginning to bud." "Why, so they are!" Fairy cried delightedly. Putting her crossed arms over her shoulders she could feel the wings curled like fern-fronds; then they began to unfold in such lustrous shimmering beauty that Streak o' Lightning turned several catherine-wheels, and folks on Earth said: "The Aurora Australis!" Fairy spread her wings in the golden air to shake out the creases, looking to right and left over her shoulders to see their loveliness. "I have almost forgotten how to fly! Oh, no, I have not!" she added hastily. "Good-bye, good-bye, Streak o' Lightning! I have begun and I cannot stop."

"Well, well!" said Streak o' Lightning, mopping his brow with his primrose bandana, "I thought *I* was swift! But Fairies certainly are the *quickest* things! There she goes like a shooting star! Now she flashes on the horizon like a peep o' rainbow! She's over the edge! Now she's in Fairyland."

The Little Green Door

But if you wish to know what Fairy saw and did in Fairyland, and how she came back sometimes to Earth, how she met the Fairy Queen, and helped Jasper and Sylvie and all her other little Earth-friends, you must ask the Fairies to close you in the ring of dream-flowers, as they did Robin and Maykin at Old Tranquillity Farm.

Beyond the little mossy door
　　There lies a sea of golden light,
And far away the shining shore
　　Of Fairyland gleams bright.
O Love is there, and Faith, and Joy,
　　And burning Hope, and radiant Truth,
And every little broken toy,
　　And the lost dreams of Youth.

Beyond the little mossy door
　　Our Fairy dreams like flowers unfold ;
And, when they waken, nevermore
　　We leave the land of gold.
The door is only Fairy size,
　　And misty mortal eyes are blind ;
But if a child has Shiny Eyes
　　The door is clear to find.

Printed by LOWE & BRYDONE (PRINTERS) LTD., London, N.W. 1